CHAMELEON

THE REAPER CHRONICLES 8

BY APRYL BAKER

CHAMELEON

LIMITLESS PUBLISHING

Limitless Publishing, LLC
Kailua, HI 96734
www.limitlesspublishing.com

Formatting: Limitless Publishing

ISBN-13: 978-1-64034-688-8

DEDICATION

For my sister.

CHAPTER ONE

Softly falling snow blankets the ground as I walk deeper and deeper into the trees. It's not long before I come upon a scene that forces my bare feet to pause in their trek.

The cabin is sitting in the middle of the woods, built right into the trees themselves. The moon's out, shining down on it, but it doesn't make it appear welcoming. Instead, it looks and feels eerie sitting there all alone. I have a bad feeling about this place.

I step to the side, hiding myself in the trees, much as the cabin appears to be doing. I'm not sure how I got here, or even

1

where this is. There are no distinguishing landmarks around me. I'm not sure I've ever been this deep in the forest before.

The cold is intense. The icicles hanging from the skeletal branches of the trees speak to the freezing temperatures. Wrapping my arms around myself, I move a little closer to the cabin, sticking to the shadows.

Why am I out here with no coat and no shoes?

Looking around, I try to understand. There's no obvious answer staring me in the face. Instead, I have the creepy cabin in the woods and the snow.

Maybe I'm dreaming. That would make sense as to why I'm out here with no winter coat or shoes.

An owl hoots in the distance, and I jump, startled at the sound. It's as loud as a gunshot in all the silence. Letting out the breath I'm holding, I look toward the cabin again. It's the only thing out here. So, if I'm dreaming, maybe I need to go investigate.

I don't want to, though. I really don't want to. Anyone who watches horror movies knows *the person who goes to investigate the creepy cabin alone, well, they die a horrible and gruesome death. Every. Single. Time.*

And that stupid owl hooting at me is not helping!

The longer I stand here, the colder I get and the creepier the cabin becomes.

It's a dream. Just go look, and I'll wake up.

Right?

Sighing, I stay hidden in the trees and move closer. The cabin doesn't get friendlier the closer I go. The logs are the same color as the trees, helping it to blend in. If I weren't hyperaware of it, I might not even notice it at first glance. I'd probably walk right past it without a thought.

There's no porch. Which is odd. I've seen very few houses in Jacob's Fork without one. Too many people love to sit in a rocking chair or porch swing around here to not have a front porch. Maybe there's a back porch.

Anything to not have to approach the front door sounds like a good idea.

Darting around the cabin proves difficult as the trees are so close together, forming a wall of sorts. The trees are acting as a fence.

I find a gap and slip through. The cold intensifies, the wind coming out of nowhere to hit me right in the face with a blast that takes my breath away. The cold is so deep, I feel it in my bones. They ache from the icy temperature. Why is it so much colder back here?

There isn't a back porch, but there is a door.

Nope, not going inside.

The ground around me is uneven, and I do my best not to fall as I go closer to the cabin. There are small mounds all over the ground back here, and I pause, paying a little more attention. The mounds go on as far as I can see, some fresh, some old, like they've become a part of the land itself.

What is this?

Squatting, I touch one of the raised mounds. At first, I think it's just dirt, but then

4

a spark, like static electricity, runs up my fingers and ripples along my arm. Jerking it back, I fall, landing on my butt.

What is this place? Scooting backward, I do my best to get away from the mounds and back into the trees. Once I reach the trunks, I pull myself up, keeping my eyes on the large anomaly stretching out before me.

The wind howls, and the cold wraps around me. My entire body aches, and I want to run away, but something holds me there. There's something here.

I wouldn't.

The scratchy words are whispered by my ear, and I jump, pushing off the tree and stumbling farther down, looking for the gap I'd slipped through before.

My head begins to hurt as the wind howls louder.

The pain starts in the center of my forehead and spreads outward until it reaches my eyes, and the pain is so bad, I fall to my knees, my hands clutching my head. It feels like someone is shoving something sharp through my skull over and over.

You need to run and never look back, that same scratchy voice whispers, and I look up through blurry eyes. The scream that leaves me echoes in the night, answered by only the hooting owl.

Where the mounds are, there is now a ghost standing above each and every one of them. All of them mangled and horribly disfigured. All of them women.

"What is this place?"

Run!

Hands push me, and I start to fall again, feeling the ghosts reach out to grab me, to keep me there. Fingers snatch at me, tangling in my hair, and before I can scream again, the world goes dark, and I open my eyes to the comfort of my own room.

I put my hand on my chest, feeling my heart beating so fast it might actually come out of my chest.

That was a weird nightmare.

One I hope never to have again.

But it was a dream, and it can stay there.

Lying back down, I close my eyes, but it's a long time before I can relax.

The sound of a hooting owl echoes as I finally fall asleep.

CHAPTER TWO

"Shortcake, whatcha over there thinking about?"

I glance at Eli, who's looking though the microscope on our lab table. He and I both have advanced biology this semester, and since I didn't know anyone else in the class, he decided we were going to be lab partners. He said Jordan could partner up with another guy on the football team. I was grateful. I didn't look forward to trying to make small talk with a stranger. There are still some in this town who think my sister

8

and I are lepers because of who our father is. Even though we cut Dad out of our lives, they blame us for the damage he did. His choices are not ours, and therefore not our fault. I wish people would understand that.

"I'm thinking I don't feel good."

"You sick?"

"I woke up with a sore throat and runny nose. I'll deal. I just don't feel good."

"Fever?"

I shake my head. At least I don't think so.

"You want to go home? I can take you during lunch."

"I have my car."

"Cecily can drive it home after school."

"She's going over to Rainelle's house after school. They've got some kind of project that has to be finished today. If I go home, I'll drive myself."

He frowns, clearly not liking that idea at all.

It's the whole kidnapping thing. No one wants to let me go anywhere by myself, and I get it. I really do, but things have to go back to normal at some point. I can't be under constant guard. That's no way to live. I think my test results prove to the Army I'm human, even if I'm a little more than that.

"Why don't you take my Jeep? It's snowing, and I don't trust your little car not to slide out of control on the roads."

"Fine, I'll take your Jeep." I love his new Jeep. Gramps bought it for him when he totaled his over Christmas. It still has that new car smell and is decked out with all the gizmos and gadgets you could want, according to Gramps. And it is. It also has brand new snow tires on it. Mine has all-weather tries, but since it's snowing outside, I'd rather have the snow tires.

"Mr. McGreggor, Miss Banks, having a nice little chat over there?" Mrs. Mullins, our biology teacher, smiles snidely. She loves calling people out.

"Actually, Ella's not feeling well. She's going to go home. I offered her my Jeep since it has snow tires." Eli smiles broadly. "I'm sure her mother will appreciate me looking out for her safety."

"Then pack up, Miss Banks, and go to the office."

She's not happy she's not going to be able to embarrass us for daring to talk during class. She's been known to make people repeat word for word what they were talking about or reading notes aloud that were passed during class. People like her who get off on power trips deserve some bad karma.

Eli hands me his keys, and I give him mine, knowing he'll bring my car home. I pack up my things and walk out of the class, going to the office to sign myself out with them warning me they were going to call my mother to let her know. Standard school policy. I might be old enough to sign myself out, but to the school, parents have a right to know.

As much as I'm getting used to the snow and the cold, my body is not as quick in adjusting. It's snowed every day for the last three weeks. There's about eight or nine inches of snow on the ground right now, and it's still snowing. Not heavy snow like we got over Christmas, but a steady, light snow that probably won't add much to the accumulation, but still enough to be annoying. The snow minus the Christmas lights has lost some of its magical appeal. Now, I'm ready to see a solid week or two of sunshine and temperatures that get out of the low twenties.

Even Gramps has been complaining about the cold. He said it hasn't been this cold or snowy in years. My first real winter in ages, and of course I get the "worst winter in years" experience.

Not that it isn't pretty, because it is. I mean where else are you going to be surrounded on all sides by mountains covered in the white stuff, looking like a painting? It's beautiful honestly. Just because I can admit that doesn't mean I don't wish the sun would stick its head out from behind the heavy snow clouds.

As I approach Eli's Jeep, I unlock it and admire the vehicle. He went back to a Jeep Grand Cherokee. Gramps offered him a Rubicon or a Wrangler, but Eli said he enjoyed the comfort of his older Cherokee.

Most guys would have been salivating at the thought of a Rubicon. And the ones we knew did. Every one of them told him he should have gotten the Rubicon, but Eli only smiled and stuck by his choice.

His new Jeep is a deep metallic blue with comfy heated seats. It also has a remote start, which is nice on cold mornings. Gramps offered to get me and Cecily a new car as well, but Mom said no. She's not comfortable letting him give us something so expensive. I think if the weather stays this nasty, she might change her mind. I won't argue. I mean, my car is older and not good on snow and ice. Mom knows this, but she refuses to ask Dad to help buy us a new car, and since she's not working full time, it's a moot point. I'm thinking of getting a job to try to save for something a little newer than what I have now. A job won't kill me, and if I want my own money when college rolls around, I need a job.

Just not sure what I want to do. I'm thinking of checking with the local bookstore to see if they need help. I love books, and it would be right up my alley. Worse comes to worst, I can always check Tazewell or Bluefield to see if anyone's hiring, like Walmart or one of the fast food places. I'd just prefer to work a little closer to home. But I guess we'll see.

Mom and Jessie's mom have decided to start their own event planning business. Gramps has encouraged it and even pushed for Mom to offer catering services. My mother is a wonderful cook who likes to make her food look pretty as well as taste good. If she can provide the food and all the other details in a one-stop-shop kind of service, she might get more business. Gramps has what he calls a chef's kitchen and said it needs to be used more.

Cecily even offered to bake all the cakes and things. Mom barely hid her grimace. My sister can cook, but she can't bake. Mom is thinking of approaching the bakery we normally use to see if they can provide all the baked goods for her new endeavor. I think it's a perfect idea.

I turn onto the road that leads to our driveway and sigh. I think I'm running a fever. My face feels hot, and all I want to do is go find some cold meds and some Tylenol. Then I want to snuggle up in bed and sleep for the rest of the day. I feel awful.

No one's home when I arrive, and I'm grateful for that. Mom would fuss over me, and Gramps would do the same, only in a gruffer manner. Like I said, I just want to sleep.

It doesn't take long to change into my PJs and take some meds. Going back upstairs, I settle down in my bed and flick on the TV, settling on *Shetland*, a British show. I've become enamored of the British crime dramas recently. Everyone else, not so much, so I tend to watch them in my room.

Yawning, I blow my nose and fight back a sneeze. I hate sneezing. It makes you feel like you have no control over yourself when you sneeze or vomit. Two of the worst things, in my opinion.

My phone chirps with a text from Eli, demanding to know I made it home. I text

15

him back a thumbs-up and set my phone on the bedside table, plugging it in to charge. Yawning, I turn off the lamp and lie back, hoping to fall asleep. I'm exhausted. My body aches, and I'm afraid I might be getting the flu. I've only had it once before when I was nine, and I remember feeling exactly like this. It was an unpleasant experience I don't relish repeating.

An hour later, I flip over and sigh. As tired as I am, I can't sleep. Throwing the covers back, I sit up and retrieve my laptop from the foot of the bed. Maybe looking at the screen can force my eyes to realize sleep is necessary for me to feel better.

I check my email, look at Instagram, and then X, formerly known as Twitter. I still call it Twitter, though. It'll always be that to me. Same old, same old on all the sites.

A knock at the door interrupts my mindless web browsing. An innate fear grips me for a heartbeat. I'm the only one home. What if it's the Army's Supernatural Containment Unit again? What if they've been watching and know I'm alone? What if they try to take me again?

My phone starts ringing. I snatch it up to keep whoever is outside from hearing it.

"What's wrong?" Eli demands. "You're so scared I can barely breathe through it."

"Someone's outside," I whisper.

"Who?"

"I don't know. They rang the doorbell, but I'm the only one here."

"They rang the doorbell." It's a statement and not a question.

"What if it's the Army?"

"I don't think they'd ring the doorbell, Shortcake."

He's right about that. Still, my instincts are telling me to run and hide.

"Look out your window and see who it is."

I crawl over to the window, the phone gripped in my hand. An old model car from the seventies is outside, so dirty I can't tell what color it is right off. The windows are tinted, and it gives me a bad feeling in the pit of my stomach. I tell Eli as much.

"It might be a Hunter looking for Gramps. They typically drive older-model cars. No electronics to track them with."

"They all have his number and would call."

A man steps off the porch, and I stay well out of sight. His shoulder-length brown hair curls at the edges, fighting with the hood of his coat. His eyes sweep the house, almost like he's looking for me, and it gives me the creeps.

"Ella?" Eli whispers, his tone matching mine. "What's going on?"

"I… He's looking at the house, like he knows I'm in here. I can't explain it, but I feel it in my bones."

"Stay inside. I'm coming."

"I'm calling the police station." I crawl back over to my nightstand where I keep my burner phone and dig it out. I don't want to hang up with Eli to call the police. I inch my way back to the window, and my panic ratchets up a notch. The car is still there, but he's not. Where did he go?

Shaking my head, I try to focus. I know the police station's number by heart and dial it quickly.

"Jacob's Fork Sheriff's Office. This is Deputy Charles. How may I help you?"

"Deputy Charles, this is Ella Banks. There's someone outside my house, and I don't recognize them or the car. I don't know where they went. I'm upstairs in my bedroom."

A loud banging comes from downstairs.

"It sounds like they're trying to get in," I whisper.

"Can you get to a locked room, Ella?"

"I can lock my bedroom door."

"Do that and then get into the closet. Keep yourself hidden. I'm sending a deputy out to you now. You're staying at Marco McGregor's place, aren't you?"

"Yes, ma'am."

"I have a deputy less than three minutes from you. Deputy Gage is on his way. What kind of car is it?"

"Old, like from the seventies. I think Dad called them muscle cars."

19

"Color?"

"It's too dirty to tell. It could be black or dark blue."

"Did you get a look at the person?"

"Tall, dark brown hair that reaches his shoulders. I don't know how old he is."

"Can you make a guess?"

"Late twenties or thirties, maybe?"

I hear the door downstairs splinter as it's forced open. It's only then I remember I didn't reset the alarm when I came in. *Stupid, stupid, stupid.*

"He's in the house."

"Is your door locked?"

"Yes."

"Go to the closet."

Yeah, no. I've seen enough horror movies to know what a big mistake that is. Hiding in obvious closets never works, especially ones in a locked room. That's how you die. Getting under the bed is an even worse idea.

A calm washes over me. Some of the debilitating fear fades simply because I know it's not the Army. I've survived them; I can survive a burglar too. I can do this. I'm a horror movie expert. I know what not to do.

Deciding on a different course of action, I open my door, turn the lock, and pull it closed softly. Then I head to Mom's room, leaving her door open, and hurry to the walk-in closet, leaving that door open as well. I fit right behind her suitcases, which are nestled under a shelf. Throwing blankets over my legs, I slink down, and I can just make out a little through the crack between the two large suitcases. Picking up the stack of blankets, I put them back beside the suitcases, effectively keeping me hidden from anyone throwing a cursory glance this way.

Footsteps echo as he walks up the stairs.

I mute my phone, turning the screen dark. The deputy will probably be mad, but I've watched enough horror films to know how to get yourself killed quickly, and I'm not doing that.

All the while, Eli has been listening on my other phone, which I've also muted and darkened the screen. He won't be mad. He might yell, but he'll understand why I did it.

The only problem with this plan is if the intruder is a shifter. He'll smell me, and all this will be for naught.

I hear him walk up and down the hall, and I see him pass by Mom's open door. He doesn't look my way, so maybe he's not a shifter. He has on dark jeans, and his sneakers are white with the Skechers logo on them. It's really all I can see from my hiding spot.

His steps aren't soft or quiet, another clue he's not a shifter. But he could be some other kind of Supernatural. Or he could just be a human who likes to break into people's houses. The normal, run-of-the-mill burglar. Or someone who has evil intentions. Human is the best bet, since he got past Gramps' wards.

I hear him trail down the hall and into the rooms. Then he gets to mine. The doorknob rattles, and I try to think if I left anything out that might make him think I'm home. Just my laptop, and the TV is on, but anyone could leave a TV on when they leave the house. Right?

My car is in the drive, though. Its presence screams, "Someone is home."

My bedroom door splinters, and I hear the wood crack as he pushes through. He's strong, suggesting…well, someone who works out to stay strong. Or a Supe. Either is possible.

It grows quiet, and I assume he's searching my room, looking for me. The thought of him going through my room is a whole other level of creepy.

His footsteps hit the hallway again, and he goes slower this time until he gets to the open doorway of Mom's room. He looks in the room and then comes inside, looking under the bed.

See? You do not hide under the bed. Horror movie 101. That gets you killed every single time.

My heartbeat speeds up when he comes over to the closet. He's so close I can smell him. It's a deep, woodsy smell mixed with something I can't identify. Something slightly bitter.

His feet shuffle into the closet, and I hold my breath, afraid to even breathe. Any sound could give me away. He turns slowly, looking at everything. I'm sort of glad I can't see his face. He starts looking behind things on the other side, and just as he reaches for the suitcases, sirens blare in the distance.

Cursing, he runs out of the closet, and it's not long before I hear the slamming of the door downstairs. A car starts, and I assume he's getting out before the police see him.

And still, I don't move, the fear from before rushing back. He was right there. Ten more seconds, and he would have found me.

"Ella Banks!" Deputy Gage calls from below. I know him. He's been over to the house with Sheriff McReynolds.

Finally, shaking my fear at the familiar voice, I tumble out of the closet.

"Here!" I call, standing on shaky legs. I unmute both phones. "Deputy Gage is here,"

I say out loud to both phones and disconnect with the sheriff's office. "Eli?"

"Almost there, Shortcake."

Nodding, I turn as Deputy Gage comes in, gun out. I flinch away from it.

"Are you hurt?" His eyes scan the room. "The front door is busted open."

"So's my bedroom door. I locked it and hid in here."

"Smart girl. Are you hurt?"

"No. Scared, but not hurt."

"Come downstairs and don't touch anything."

I quirk a brow. I live here. My prints are on everything. He seems to realize what he said and shakes his head.

"I have more units on the way. Did you see the intruder?"

I nod. "Not well, but Gramps has cameras everywhere. One of them probably caught him."

"Go downstairs and wait in Gramps' office," Eli says. "I'll be there in five minutes."

I can do that. I follow the deputy as he goes back down the stairs, and then I take a seat on the couch across from Gramps' desk.

It's only then the shaking starts. I reach over and grab a throw, pulling it around me. Eli will be here soon.

I'm safe.

The shaking doesn't subside, and I think it's shock.

Pulling the throw tighter, I take deep breaths and try to stay calm.

Eli will be here soon.

I can deal until then.

I think.

CHAPTER THREE

Eli arrives a lot faster than I thought he would. He bursts through the door, his eyes almost glowing with the Guardian Angel blood running through his veins. He really is beautiful. I know guys hate to be called that, but it's the only real word to describe Eli McGreggor.

At eighteen, you can't quite call him a man, but he's not a boy either. He's at that in-between stage. Despite his football physique, he still has a little of that baby face going on. Blond hair stands on end like he's been running his hands through it, and it gives a stark contrast to his dark aqua eyes. He's gotten taller since I met him as well. He stands well over six feet. Gramps says it's due to him taking on the mantle of Guardian Angel. That blood made his body into a weapon to protect me. It's also a good thing for his football career. Let's be real. How many football players are short? Not that many.

He drops to his knees in front of me and looks me over from head to toe. "Did he touch you?"

I shake my head. "No, I hid in Mom's closet, but he was there, about to pull the suitcases away when he heard the sirens."

"Good girl. I was afraid you'd hide in your closet."

"Not likely. I watch too many horror movies for that. It would have been the dumbest thing I could have done. I locked my door and went to Mom's room. I fit right behind her suitcases."

"Pays to be a shortcake every now and then, doesn't it?"

Normally, I don't mind my stature despite my sister's Amazon warrior height. Sometimes I do hate it, but today was not one of those days.

"*Ella!*" Mom screams as she comes into the house. "*Ella!*"

"We're in the office, Mrs. B," Eli calls, but he doesn't move from where he's on his knees. "Are you okay?"

"I'm shaking."

"Not as bad as when you slipped into that dream with the Sandman. And you're talking, so your shock isn't as bad either."

"Do we need an ambulance?" Deputy Gage looks up from where he's sitting at Gramps' desk.

"I think we should probably get her checked out," Eli says just as Mom comes barreling into the room, her eyes wide and frightened. She rushes over and pulls me up into a hug, her own body shaking worse than mine.

"Ella Grace, you and your sister are going to put me into an early grave."

"Mom, it wasn't my fault someone broke into the house."

"No, no, of course not," she hurries to say. "I'm just being a worried mother. None of this is your fault." She hugs me tighter.

"The ambulance is on the way," Deputy Gage says and hangs up the phone.

"Ambulance…" Mom pulls away from me and looks me over as carefully as Eli did. "Are you hurt?"

"She's in shock." Eli gently extracts me from Mom's hold and sits me back down, pulling the blanket around me. "I asked for an ambulance because she needs to be checked out." He grabs the throw pillows and has me lie back so he can put my feet up. We've all learned how to treat shock over the last few months.

"Ella, we're going to need a formal statement once you're medically cleared." Deputy Gage stands. "Ma'am, we're going to ask that you all stay in here until forensics go through the house looking for evidence and fingerprinting surfaces. The state police are sending a team from Welch to help out with the investigation."

"Might want to call Cecily and have her stay with Rainelle tonight." Eli tucks the blanket around me. "I'll call Gramps and have him get someone out here to fix the front door."

"And my room."

Mom looks at me sharply. "Your room?"

"He broke down my door as well."

Her gasp is loud enough to be heard outside. "Did he hurt you?"

"No, I made him think I was in there and hid in your room."

"Good girl." Mom sighs heavily. "Any idea who it was?"

"I've never seen him before."

Before I can say anything else, more sirens break the quiet of afternoon, and we're flooded with more police, and then the sheriff hustles in. Ethan McReynolds is a wolf shifter and an Alpha in his own right. Cole Walker might be the Alpha of the new shifter clan, but Ethan is still a leader of the wolves. Cole didn't take that from him, and I'm glad.

His dark hair and brown eyes are concerned when he sees me. "Ella Grace, are you all right? Were you hurt?"

"No, just shock, I think."

He nods. "Ambulance should be here soon. Forensics should be here soon as well. Gage, I'll want your report as the first responder on my desk before the end of your shift."

"Yes, sir."

Ethan comes over and sits on the coffee table. "Now, Ella, I know you're not up to questions, but we'll need a formal statement soon. People tend to forget details the longer we wait to interview them."

"I already told the deputy everything I remember."

He smiles slightly. "You'd be surprised at what you might remember when retelling it later."

"Didn't you just say people tend to forget and not remember?"

He laughs. "It's a fine line. Both can be true. Did you see anything before the intruder came in the house? A vehicle…"

"I saw his car, but all I can tell you is it's an old muscle car from the seventies. I don't know a make or model outside of that."

His body tenses, and my hackles rise. What does he know?

"What color was it?"

"Could have been black or dark blue. It was too dirty to really tell."

He stands and walks out of the room. Eli follows him without my having to ask. He picked up on Ethan's weird behavior too.

Mom frowns after him but doesn't follow. There's something about the way she's staring at the doorway that sets my teeth on edge. Ethan's been coming around a lot more than he used to. You don't think…

"Mom?"

"Yes, honey?"

"What's going on with you and the sheriff?"

She startles at my question, looking very much like a deer in the headlights.

"Nothing."

"I call BS."

"Ella, I wouldn't lie to you about that. There's nothing going on between us. He's just been a really good friend to me since your father left our lives. I'm not sure I'd have made it through without someone to talk to. He's been through the same thing."

"What do you mean?"

"I'm not sure I'd should say. It was something private he shared with me, and he's still hurting over it."

"Was he married?"

"Once upon a time."

Now, that's news. Gramps will tell me. Ethan's a shifter, and I don't want Mom falling for him when he'll drop her like a hot potato if he meets his mate. She'll be heartbroken. When my mother loves, she loves with her entire being, and the mate bond will shatter that.

I decided to tell Cecily about Leo, her mate, over the Christmas holiday. It's been bothering me, and the more I've thought about it, the more I think she has a right to know. I've seen how strong that bond is. Jason Blackburne Reed is mated to Eli's sister, Ava. After observing them together, I can't not tell my sister. I just hope she understands why I kept it from her, why we all did.

"The ambulance is here," Mom murmurs. "Let me go get them…"

"No, Deputy Gage said to stay here. The cops will escort them back. We don't want to contaminate any evidence."

Mom nods and fidgets with her hands, staring off into space.

"Mom? You okay?"

She sighs. "I'm tired, sweetheart, and scared. Someone was in our home, and they could have hurt you. I don't know if we should go somewhere else for the night or until they catch whoever this was."

"Chances are they won't catch him," I inform her and pull my blanket tighter. "Ninety percent of break-ins aren't solved. It's a statistical fact."

"I doubt they live in a town of Supernaturals."

She's got me there.

"You don't seem to be shaking as badly as you were." Mom goes to sit down at the end of the couch and decides better. The EMTs will probably make her move.

I *am* feeling better, and I think she's right. I'm not shaking as much. I guess talking to my mommy and knowing she's here made the difference. No matter who you are or how old you are, when something bad happens, you want your mom. I'll call you a liar to your face if you say you don't.

The EMTs come in and give me a once-over, agreeing my symptoms are shock, but they appear to be getting better. They don't think I need to go to the hospital since I'm already doing everything they would. I didn't argue because I hate the hospital. I've seen too much of that place since arriving in Jacob's Fork, West Virginia.

Once they clear out, Mom forces Ethan to let her into the kitchen to make me a cup of tea. Lemon tea with honey. It's my favorite. Yes, there's a little sugar in it, but my system needs it right now. I'm diabetic, but I can have a little sugar here and there.

I'm sitting there, my hands wrapped around the warm mug, when Eli comes back in. He frowns, seeing me sitting up instead of lying down, but I shake my head. "I'm feeling better. If my symptoms start to come back, I'll lie down. I need to drink something hot."

"Fine, but you need to stay put."

"What was up with Ethan?"

He closes his eyes and sighs heavily. "There's been a string of break-ins across Mercer, McDowell, Tazewell, Wyoming, and Buchannon Counties over the last few months."

"They think this is the guy?"

"Ella, wait. They were targeted break-ins."

"Targeted?"

"Women alone."

My eyes widen, and a lead weight drops in my stomach. "Were they…?"

"Raped, yeah. And killed."

"We would have heard about that on the news."

"They're keeping it out of the news, or at least they're trying to so they stand a better chance of catching the guy."

"That's stupid. People need to know about the danger."

"I agree, but not my call. From what they know, the guy stalks his victims, learns their habits, and eventually kills them. You're hardly ever alone. I think he saw his chance today and took it."

"How do they know this is him?" My throat tightens, and I feel the first signs of hysteria creeping up. "It could just be a random break-in…"

"The car, Ella. That car has been seen in the vicinity of all the murders. It was him. Ethan's going through our security footage now trying to get an image of him and a plate number."

"The Ring camera…"

"The car wasn't parked near the porch. It was just out of range. When he broke down the door, he never looked up. There's not a clear image of his face."

Ethan comes in, followed by Mom, who has gone so pale, I think she's in need of sugar more than me.

"Ella, has Eli filled you in on what's going on?"

I nod woodenly, my stomach in knots. I feel sick. He's been following me?

"Can you think back over the last few weeks and try to remember if you ever saw that car or him in your vicinity?"

"I didn't recognize him or the car, so I don't think so."

He sighs. "I'm going to assign a deputy at your school, and we'll have one stationed here at the house who's going to shadow you until we find him."

Normally, I'd argue, but I'd been in the same room with him. I knew something felt off about him, something that scared me. I'll take all the protection I can get.

"Maybe it'll scare him off?" Mom asks. "He'll go away and leave Ella alone?"

Ethan doesn't comment, and Eli doesn't look like he agrees. He knows more about this stuff since his dad is an FBI agent who handles serious crimes, mostly dealing with Supes, but serious, nonetheless.

"You're going to be fine, Ella. I promise."

"Cops never make promises."

Ethan smiles. "Most cops aren't shifters. The deputy assigned to you is going to be a shifter. He'll smell him before he gets near you."

I hope so.

Stalker, rapist, and murderer.

Only in this town.

"It's going to be fine," Mom tries to assure me, but I think it's more for her than me. She looks like she's ready to drop.

"Mom, why don't you go make yourself some tea and eat something?"

"No…"

"She's right, Molly," Ethan says gently. "You need to get some sugar in you before *you* go into shock."

Eli narrows his eyes, seeing what I saw, only this time from Ethan.

Yeah, we need to sit and have a chat with the good sheriff.

After they catch this serial killer.

Ethan takes Mom by the arm and leads her out of the room, probably toward the kitchen.

"That's a problem," Eli mutters. "We have enough problems without that particular one."

"You're telling me," I whisper.

"Hey, they're right about one thing. You're going to be fine. I'm not letting you out of my sight. We're going to be glued at the hip until they get him."

I hope so.

"Gramps arranged for us all to stay over at the inn tonight. They can't get here to fix the door until tomorrow, and he refuses to let 'the women' stay in an unsafe house. His words, not mine."

"I don't really want to stay here, anyway."

"Cecily is staying with Rainelle. She's probably blowing up your phone, but I assured her you were good."

At least she's safe tonight.

"Come on, Shortcake, drink your tea, and let's go pack a bag. The sooner we get you out of here, the faster you're going to calm down."

Again, I hope so.

Dutifully, I do as he asks, then follow him upstairs to pack a bag and grab my school stuff. But I can't go in. The sight of my door hanging off the hinges only serves to remind me of what I escaped.

"Hey, it's okay." He pushes me toward his room and then settles me down on the bed. "I'll get some stuff for you. That good with you?"

I nod, curling up on his bed. I feel safer in his room.

It only takes a few minutes for him and Mom to get everything together, and then we leave the house in the police's hands. Ethan promised to board up the door before he left.

A serial killer.

What's next?

It's not a question I want to answer.

CHAPTER FOUR

It took a bit to get everyone settled into our rooms. Mom wanted us to have rooms side by side or connecting, if possible, but it wasn't possible. She ended up on the other end of the hall. The place was booked with people who came to ride on the Hatfield and McCoy Trail. The inn was popular with tourists because they had a place to lock up the four wheelers while not in use. It made the visitors feel better, knowing their property was secured behind a locked garage door.

Snowy Ridge Inn is a new building, but it was designed with the mountain environment in mind just like all the other buildings in town. There's lots of stone and wood, but with all the modern amenities, including extremely good Wi-Fi. The room is cozy, a plushy rug between the two queen beds inviting you to squish your toes in it. Did I mention I love fluffy or furry rugs?

Eli is lying on his bed looking through his phone, and he seems more lost in thought than actually paying attention to what he's doing. He's been like this since before we left the house. It makes me think he knows something he's keeping from me, and I don't like it. But it could be something personal he doesn't want to share about his family or something, and I don't want to push.

"Kids?" Mom calls through the door, and I get up to let her in. We'd locked the inside locks just in case.

"Hey, Mom." I stand back to let her in. She's carrying bags from the new Chinese place in town. It smells divine.

"Thought you might be hungry. Ethan picked it up for us. He remembered you loved the soup from there."

There is Ethan's name again.

"Mom, you do know Ethan's a shifter, right?"

"Of course." She sits the bags down on the small table and turns to me. "Why do you ask?"

"It's just…"

"It's just?" she prompts when my words fall away.

What if I'm wrong? I mean, I don't think she'd jump into another relationship when her divorce isn't even final.

"It's just we're worried," Eli says after a moment.

"Worried?" Mom looks so confused. "About what?"

"Shifters mate for life." Eli tosses his phone on the bed and comes over to help put the food out. "When they meet their mate, it doesn't matter who they might be in a relationship with or how much they might care. A mate bond trumps everything."

45

"Why are you telling me this?"

"Because we've noticed Ethan's been hanging around a lot, and you two seem to be overly friendly." Eli puts it out there without a trace of emotion.

Her eyes widen. "Do you two think he and I…that we're…"

We both nod.

"Ethan is my friend who has been there for me through all of this. I owe him so much when it comes to you and Cecily. His pack has done everything they can to protect you both. Because of that, we're very close."

"It seems like he might want to be more than that." I pick up a paper plate and start loading food onto it.

She pauses in picking up her own plate and frowns. "Do you think so?"

"Which is why we're worried." Eli takes his own plate and sits down on the bed. "We don't want to see you get invested and him hurt you when and if he meets his mate."

"I'm not ready for a relationship yet," Mom says firmly. "The divorce isn't even final. I would never break my marriage

46

vows until those papers are signed. Neither of you should worry. And if I ever choose to start a relationship with Ethan, I'd go into it eyes wide open, understanding the mate bond would always be a possibility."

Does that mean she's thought about it? Or did we make her think about it by suggesting Ethan wanted more than friendship? Oops.

"But, Mom…"

"Don't 'but Mom' me, Ella Grace. I'm a grown woman, and I can see who I want. Now, eat. You need food in you after the shock you've had."

My mother basically just told me to mind my own business when I'm only trying to look out for her. She's right, though. She *is* a grown woman who has her own thoughts and feelings. She's my mom, but she's her own person too.

"Now, I'm going back to my room. I have some phone calls to make about an event we're putting together for the hospital. If you need me, text me and I'll come running."

Mom lets herself out, and Eli and I both sigh heavily.

"I think maybe we shouldn't have said anything to Mama Molly." Eli frowns at the door. "We put the idea in her head."

"That's what I thought too. We should have talked to Ethan about our concerns instead of Mom."

We made it a bigger mess than it was.

"Hindsight and all that," I mutter and pick up the large container of soup. There are no bowls. Eli hands me a plastic spoon.

"Might as well drink it," he says with a laugh when I make a face at how small the spoon is. "I'm not going to eat it, and I bet Molly has her own food in her room."

Shrugging, I do as he suggests, which makes him laugh harder. Hey, it's good soup. A person could chug it and die happy.

Once we'd eaten and put the leftovers away in the fridge—yes, the rooms have a full-size fridge—Eli turns serious.

"Shortcake, there's something we need to talk about. There's more to what Ethan told us at the house, and I've been debating on telling you or not."

"If it's about my safety, then I need to know."

He sighs. "The man who was at the house, there's a problem."

"Problem?" How much bigger of a problem could there be than him breaking in and trying to rape and murder women?

"None of the shifters could pick up his scent."

"Huh?" That's not possible. Every single person has a unique scent. My ex-boyfriend, who was a shifter, explained it to me. He said I smelled of strawberries and fresh cream. Which was weird because I don't even eat strawberries and cream. Too much sugar for my diabetic self.

"He searched the property himself, looking for a trace of a scent. If it wasn't for the video, he wouldn't even know the guy was there."

"That's not possible."

"I know, which is why we're all concerned. I'm torn between asking my dad to see if he's ever come across anything like this guy or not. On one hand, he might have the answers. On the other, it could bring him here to town. No one wants that. As much as I love Dad, I also know he doesn't truly see the difference between a good Supe and a bad one. He'll utilize them when he needs to, but I don't think he'll ever call one a friend."

"Isn't your sister mated to a shifter?"

He nods. "Dad hates it. He did everything he could to keep her away from Jason, but that bond is too strong. If it were up to him, she'd still be in North Carolina and dating a nice normal guy, preferably one who plans on hunting us down."

Over the last few months, Eli has started to refer to himself as a Supe, which is good. Because he is one. He's an Angel in a very human body who can morph into something more when necessary. He's been more at peace in his own skin since he accepted that.

"Gramps will figure it out. It's best not to bring Special Agent James Malone to Jacob's Fork unless absolutely necessary."

"We'll try that first, but if it gets to a point where we're out of options, I'll bring him here to keep you safe."

"But will everyone else be safe?"

He shakes his head mulishly. "You're my top priority, Ella. I can't think of everyone else. Our bond won't let me."

"That's not really fair."

"No, but it is what it is."

"Do you ever regret that you're my Guardian?"

His head snaps up, his eyes wide. "Why would you even ask me that?"

I shrug and look away. "It seems to have cost you a lot."

"No, no, it hasn't. It gave me back my life. I was dead, Shortcake. Good and truly dead. I don't remember anything about being dead, but I know I was. My last memory is of looking up into my father's face, hearing Mattie's voice, and knowing I died protecting her. If I resented anyone, it would be her, because I had to die to keep her safe. And I don't resent her. I'd do it again, same as I would for you. Don't you ever think I

51

resent you or regret being your Guardian. Got it?"

"Yeah." Still, a small part of me has to wonder, and maybe it always will. Dad and Uncle Tony forced doubts into my mind about the men in my life who are supposed to care about me. I'm not sure it'll ever really go away.

"So, what are they planning on doing to catch this guy if they can't track him?"

"Good old fashioned police work?" Eli smiles slightly. "I think they've learned to rely on their supernatural senses so much they're at a loss now that those are useless with this unsub."

"Unsub?"

"Unknown subject. It's a term the FBI uses. Have you not watched *Criminal Minds*?"

I shake my head.

"I know what we're doing this weekend."

My phone rings, and I recognize Ethan's number.

"Hello?"

"Ella, how are you?"

"Fine." My tone is a little clipped with him, but I'm worried about Mom.

"I want to come by if you're up to it and get your official statement and have you sit with a sketch artist to try to come up with a composite of the suspect we can send out to the surrounding counties."

"I can do that. We need to talk about something, anyway."

"Is everything all right?"

"I don't know, but I don't want to talk about it over the phone."

"I'll be there in half an hour or so."

"Talk soon."

"Ethan?" Eli asks.

"He's coming by to get my statement, and he wants me to sit down with a sketch artist."

"That's a good idea while the image of the guy is fresh in your mind. If we can get his picture out there, it'll help us track him."

"Us? Last I checked, you were a high school football star, not a police officer."

He shrugs. "I could be a cop, easy. I was trained by the best. And in this instance, I'm not leaving your, Cecily's, and Molly's safety in the hands of cops who are at a loss."

It actually makes me feel safer knowing he's going to be searching as well. He's the one person, besides my mother and my sister, who truly has my best interest at heart. Well, Gramps and Jamie too, but outside of them, I don't trust anyone else to do that.

"You finish eating while I take a shower, 'kay?"

"Yeah. Go on. I'll be fine."

He ruffles my hair, grabs a change of clothes, and shuts himself in the bathroom. The shower turns on, and I go back to the plate still sitting in front of me.

Nothing else to do until Ethan arrives.

CHAPTER FIVE

Ethan arrives a short while later with an older woman in tow. She has long silver hair and the brightest green eyes I've ever seen. Her face is wrinkle free, but she holds an air of wisdom about her I'd associate with my elders.

"Ella, this is Maggie McGraw. She's a local artist who fills in as a sketch artist for several counties, both in West Virginia and Virginia."

She smiles warmly at me. "I heard you had a bit of a scary adventure earlier."

"A bit," I agree, liking her instantly. She reminds me of my grandmother, who we haven't seen in over a year. Makes me miss her. Her health prevents her from traveling. Maybe I can convince Mom to go see her and Grandpa over spring break.

"Shall we sit and you tell me what you remember about him?"

"I'm not very good at art, so I don't know how good I'll be at describing him outside of some generic details."

"I'm a bit psychic, so I'll be able to see him as you think of him. It'll help me get an initial image and then you can look at what I've done and make changes based on your memories."

"Oh."

Of course the sketch artist would be psychic.

She laughs softly. "I heard that."

"I'm sorry," I sputter. She can hear my thoughts?

"Only because they're so loud and I've opened myself up to hearing them. Normally, I keep my abilities out of other people's business. Though, sometimes, when people are really emotional, they broadcast. That's part of the reason I typically stay home and away from people."

"That's sad."

She nodded. "Aye, but it gives me peace of mind, and I'll take a quiet existence over friends any day."

"I'd hate to live like that."

"You get used to it." She kicks her shoes off, goes over to the bed, and sits. "Come. Let's get this started so we can get the word out to the other police departments in the area. It might save someone's life."

Nervously, I follow her over to the bed, aware of Ethan and Eli watching us. I really am not very good at art. I can't even draw a straight line with a ruler, much to the frustration of every art teacher I've ever had.

"Don't pay attention to them. Just tell me about what happened."

Frowning, I glance at Eli, who nods. "Start from when you heard the car pull up and how it made you feel. It'll help Ms. McGraw center her thoughts on yours.

Close your eyes and think about everything."

"And I'll record it and make it your written statement as well. I'll type it up at the station and have you sign it."

I don't really want to relive it, but she's right. It might save someone's life to get a picture of the creep circulating throughout the area. And if it keeps me from having to go over this again with Ethan, that's a win.

So instead of starting with my first sighting of the car, I start at school, telling them about being sick and coming home.

"Did you notice anyone following too close when you left school?" Ethan has his notebook and pen out, scribbling away.

"No. I didn't feel good, and all my focus was on getting home. I wasn't really paying attention to if anyone was behind me."

Something I need to change. Especially after being taken by the Army. I should know better than to be unaware of my surroundings. Eli seems to agree, if his expression is anything to go by. I'm getting a lecture later. Probably from him and Gramps both.

Closing my eyes, I recall that paralyzing fear, thinking it was the Army coming to take me while no one else was home. That fear is always going to be with me. My therapist thinks I need to embrace it and use it. She's right, but it's hard. To fight through that fear is almost as bad as the fear itself.

Instead of focusing on that, I start to describe everything from the moment I called Eli to when the police showed up. It took longer than I thought it would, thanks to a few helpful questions from Ethan. He actually made me remember details I didn't think I knew. It must be a police technique they use to pull out forgotten memories from victims of crimes.

It takes a little over an hour to go through it all, and throughout everything, Ms. McGraw has been working, her eyes never leaving her sketchpad. When she shows the drawing to me, I let out a gasp my mother would be proud of.

There he is, staring back at me from the page. Not in color, but it's him all the same. She'd really captured his likeness in a way that seemed to almost come alive on the page. The only thing a little off is the eyes, which need to be a little wider. She makes the change, and I can't believe it.

"Is that him?" Ethan asks after a few minutes of me just staring at the drawing.

I nod.

"Ella, you have to speak your answer for the recording."

"Oh, sorry. Yes, it's him."

Eli snaps a photo of the sketch, which earns a frown from Ethan.

He shrugs and puts his phone back on the table. "I need to know who to look for."

Ethan stops his recording app and puts his own phone back in his pocket. "Maggie, I appreciate you coming out and doing this for us."

She smiles. "It's my pleasure. If I'm not needed any longer, I'm going to go home and drink a cup of herbal tea to calm my nerves."

"Of course," Ethan says. "I'll be right back, Ella. I want to walk Maggie to her car."

I nod, and Eli reaches out to rest his hand against my forehead. "You have a fever."

"I told you I didn't feel good. I think I'm getting the flu."

He flies to the other side of the room so fast I laugh. "Not a fan of the flu?"

He shakes his head. "I ended up getting it seven times the winter I was fourteen. I've gotten my flu shot every year without fail since then."

"Then you should be fine if you've already had it."

"Maybe," he says skeptically. "And maybe I'll buy a pack of masks when I go get you some Tylenol Cold and Flu."

He's being ridiculous, but then again, the thought of the one time I had the flu is enough to send me spiraling. I can't imagine having gotten it seven times in one season.

Ethan knocks and reenters the room. Eli looks up, startled, realizing no one had locked the door. I didn't because I knew the sheriff was coming back. Eli simply forgot. I would laugh at his expression if I didn't think he'd pout like a baby the rest of the night, and I'm the one who has to put up with him.

"Now, Ella, what did you want to talk to me about?" The sheriff settles himself into chair and sniffs. "You two have enough to eat? I wasn't sure how much to buy since neither of you are shifters, but I know football players can pack away quite a bit as well."

"Yes, thank you," I say, remembering my manners. "The food was very much appreciated. Eli was starved."

"You don't look so good, Ella. Are you all right?"

"Just sick. I think I'm getting the flu."

"She has a fever," Eli tells him.

"I've never had the flu. Shifters don't really get sick with the normal, everyday stuff."

I wouldn't call the flu normal, everyday stuff, but I'm not a shifter either.

"So, what did you want to talk about?"

"I want to talk about my mom."

"Your mother? Is something wrong?"

"Yeah, something's wrong." If I do this, Mom is going to be pissed, but it's for her own good. I think.

"What?" he prompts when I don't say anything else, real concern deepening the color of his eyes.

"We've noticed how much time you've been spending with her," Eli says. "We're worried she'll get hurt."

His eyes widen when he understands immediately what we're saying. "I promise you, I have no intention of ever hurting Molly. I can't."

"What do you mean, you can't?" I demand. "If you get involved with her and then meet your mate, you won't be able to help yourself. That whole mate bond thingy."

"*She's* my mate."

Eli and I rear back like we've been slapped.

"Excuse me?"

Ethan sighs. "I haven't told your mother. She's not ready to hear it yet."

"Uh, I'm not ready to hear it either. Explain yourself. We've been here for almost a year, and you've never even hinted at anything like this."

"That's because she was happily married, and I'm not the type of person to wreck a home just because I want something. I was raised better than that."

He looks appalled I'd even think it.

"I did my best to keep tabs on her to make sure she was safe, but I kept my distance out of respect for her marriage. She truly seemed happy, and my only real wish is for her happiness. Your father made her happy."

"Until he didn't."

Ethan nods. "For now, I'm just here for her. I'm her friend. She needs time to heal and get past the hurt Henry caused her. I have all the time in the world."

"But she doesn't," I point out. "She's human."

He smiles. "Yes, but once we claim our mates, there are ways around that."

"You mean a spell or something?"

"Or something. Her life will be tied to mine, and she'll live as long as I do with a simple spell."

"Yeah, but what if she doesn't want that?"

"Then we'll do a reverse spell, and I'll tie my life to hers. I'll live as long as she does."

"You won't age, though."

"Shifters age, just a lot slower than humans."

"My point is, she'll grow old and you won't."

"And that won't change how I feel about her."

"It might change how she feels, though, as she gets older and you don't. People will assume you're her son or grandson or something."

"I will do what Molly wants, but it's a risk I'm willing to take. Your mother's worth it."

"Of course she's worth it."

"Above all else, I want her to be happy, and if she doesn't choose me, I'll deal with it, but it won't stop me from keeping eyes on her to make sure she's happy."

65

"The way Leo does with Cecily?"

"Exactly."

"All the wolves know about Cecily being his mate. Do they know about Mom?"

Ethan nods. "They consider her part of our pack now and will keep her safe."

Well, there's that, at least. I'm not sure how I feel about Ethan claiming my mother is his mate, but honestly, she could do a lot worse. As long as he doesn't rush her, and is sincere about wanting what's best for her, I'm not going to pitch a fit. He is a good man. I've seen it time and time again.

"Okay, then. As long as you don't hurt her, we're good, but I swear by all that's holy and unholy, if you do, there's not a place you'll be able to hide from me."

"Or me and Gramps," Eli chimes in.

"I promise, Ella Grace, I'm going to do everything in my power not to hurt her."

"Then we're good."

He leaves not long after, and Eli turns to me. "So, are you good?"

"I mean, no, but it could be worse."

"Worse?"

"What if she was mated to a zombie or something?"

He snorts. "Don't speak it, for it shall come to pass. We don't need that."

I yawn. I'm so tired.

"Tell you what. You get some sleep, and I'll head over to Walgreens and get you some cold medicine."

"Can you get me some of those cherry throat drops too? My throat aches."

"Sure thing, Shortcake. Do you want me to bring you some of that cherry pop you like so well?"

"Yeah. My granny always said that if you have a sore throat to drink red pop. Not sure why, but it does make it feel better."

He points to his head. "It's all in your head. There's no reason for that to work."

"Maybe."

He ruffles my hair. "Get some sleep. I'll be back as fast as I can. Want me to get you some soup from the Coffee Shoppe?"

"Please."

"I'll let your mom know I'm leaving so she can listen for you." He stands and goes to the door. "Lock this behind me."

Doing as he asks, I go back to bed and crawl under the blankets, relishing how soft everything is. I'm exhausted, and it doesn't take long for me to fall asleep.

CHAPTER SIX

I'm not sure how long I managed to sleep, but the room is dark when I wake up. Doesn't mean it's dark outside, only that the room is dark. It takes a minute for me to remember where I am and why I'm here.

Stalker serial killer.

How in the world did I get the attention of someone like that? I mean, sure, I can be feisty and rather loud when I want to get my point across, but I'd think that would make this kind of depraved lunatic steer clear of me. Wouldn't they want the quieter, meeker

69

people? Ones who won't scream bloody murder and do as they're told? Not to say those women deserve it, because they don't. They're just more likely to be victims.

But I've been a victim before, too, so I should know better than to stereotype victims. I guess I'm just trying to rationalize the irrational because this doesn't make sense to me. Where did I even come across this guy? I've been a homebody lately, not really going anywhere except school, the diner, and the bakery. Unless he was in one of those three places, there's absolutely zero chance he saw me.

And there's the matter of his car. Ethan knew exactly which car I was talking about when I described it. He and the rest of the deputies would have been on high alert for that car. Surely, they'd have seen it in and around town. Unless he rented a car or had a second car he drove while stalking his victims. The thought makes me nervous. He hasn't been caught, and it's been months since the first attack. Chances are he's really good at what he does. Which means he's used to getting away with his crimes.

No offense to Ethan and the sheriff's department, but Eli is right. I think they have gotten so used to relying on their keen sense of smell to track down offenders, they might be at a loss as to how to deal with this particular psycho. Where does that put me? Somewhere not very safe. Even with a deputy around twenty-four-seven, if they can't smell the guy, what can they do? I mean, I might be wrong and they might have a very keen sense of observation and see him lurking, but they haven't so far. He's been stalking me, and not one officer noticed him. Who knows how long he's been in town?

It's a scary thought.

I should get up and take a shower. It might make me feel better. Currently, I feel like crap. My nose is running. My throat hurts, and my whole body aches. And I'm cold. Even with the blankets pulled up around me, I'm freezing. It feels like the flu. Just my luck I'm getting stalked and I'm sick as a dog. I should probably go to urgent care or something and get that Tamiflu stuff. If you catch it early enough, it works miracles, or at least that's what doctors always say.

Yawning, I go to sit up and then go completely still.

I heard something.

Slowly, pulling the blanket down, I look around the darkened room, but I can't detect anything out of the ordinary. The door is locked on the inside with that hook lock most hotel rooms have, and a bolt lock in addition to the electronic lock. They take their security seriously here.

What had I heard, though? I can't even define it. Just a sense of a sound that was wrong in the stillness of the dark. I glance over at the window, which has the blackout curtains closed tight. We're on the third floor, so I doubt someone climbed up there without being noticed. I look toward the door, but it's dark enough I can't see the locks. Is it still locked? It has to be. I'd have to physically pull the hook lock back even if someone got through the electronic lock and the bolt lock.

Shhhhh.

It came from right beside me, whispered in my ear.

Turning my head, it's all I can do not to scream.

Lying right next to me is a woman whose face is so badly beaten, I can barely tell her gender. Her left eye is swollen shut, the black-and-blue color stark against the paleness of her skin. Her other eye is wide open and staring at me. The blue orb is full of fear. Her lip is busted on one side, but the other side is hanging off her face, like someone tried to cut her bottom lip off and didn't get to finish the job. One ear is gone, and the gaping hole where it should be glares at me.

I start to open my mouth to scream, but she shakes her head and places a finger against her broken lips. Then she points to the door. I cover my mouth with my hand to try and keep the scream in. She doesn't mean me any harm. I think she's trying to help me.

There's that sound again. It's coming from the door. Is someone outside my door trying to get in? What are they doing to make that odd noise? It's not like they have a key, so what are they attempting to do?

I fight the urge to go look. But I do slowly reach over and grab my cell off the bedside table, silencing it so as not to alert whoever is at my door I know they're there. Or maybe they don't care if I know. I'm not sure, but I quickly text Eli that someone is outside the room and I'm being super quiet so as not to alert them I'm awake. They may not think I'm in here since Eli's gone and they just want a look around. I don't know. Either way, I don't want to make any noise.

Next, I text Mom to see where she is. It only takes a moment for her to text back that she's on the phone. I give her a thumbs-up and tell her I'll come to her room in a bit. Hopefully, it'll keep her inside. If I tell her someone's outside my door, she'll rush out and end up getting hurt or possibly taken. Not happening on my watch.

Ethan is my last text. It's a simple 9-1-1 at the inn.

And all the while, I've kept one eye on the ghost lying beside me. She's creeping me out with how still and quiet she is. Her naked body is a mess of multi-colored bruises, and several of her limbs are bent at odd angles. This woman went through a horrific nightmare before she died. She has to be one of the stalker's victims. If this is what he did to her, I want him nowhere near me.

Eli has also warned me that ghosts that die in such a brutal way can be very angry and lash out. Since I can see and hear her, I'm a likely target. So far, there have been very few experiences I've had with ghosts that are anything but heartbreakingly tragic outside of the scary little creatures in the woods and that one ghost at Lake Cree. Not gonna dismiss his warnings, though. She might be here to help me one second and turn on me the next. Best to keep a healthy dose of skepticism.

Oddly, the panic from earlier is absent. Perhaps because I know this isn't the Army.

I can deal with the fear of a stalker serial killer better than I can my fear of the Army. Then again, I remember every detail of the horrors I went through at their hands. And even though I can see the damage done to this ghost, I still fear the Army more. Weird, isn't it?

Doesn't mean I'm not terrified of who is outside my door. Because I do know what he's done. I'm looking at his handiwork. At least, I think.

And what the heck is that noise? It's like a sliding crunch. Which doesn't make sense. He's not trying to break down the door. Frankly, if he does, I know someone will come running. Shifters own and run the inn. They'd hear him and be here within seconds.

That noise is bugging me.

I turn over carefully, doing my best to not let the mattress make a sound, and look toward the door. The light from the hallway is a solid line beneath the door, only broken by the silhouette of someone standing out there. I can see his shoes.

Slide. Crunch. Crunch. Slide.

What is that?

It's how he got into my house.

I nearly scream as her broken and hoarse voice scrapes against the inside of my skull.

But what *is it?*

I forget I can talk to them with the mental connection we share. It sure does come in handy at times like these.

I don't know. I remember hearing it too.

Well, that's just dandy, as Gramma Banks would say.

Sirens start to wail in the distance, and I wince. There went the element of surprise. Sure enough, I hear footsteps running down the hall. Why would Ethan come in sirens blaring? He should know better.

We should be safe now… I turn to look at the ghost, but it's no longer just her. Two more girls are standing there with her. They all have red hair.

I have red hair.

He's into redheads? Is this how he chooses his victims? Not good, not good at all. I'm dying my hair back to blonde.

Shaking my head, I focus on the women. They're just as brutalized as she is, and my heart breaks for them. They're all young as well. I'd guess the oldest is no more than twenty, and the youngest maybe fifteen if I push the limits of my imagination. She might be twelve, for all I know.

You're next, the youngest says, her wide gray eyes fixed on me with a maniacal intent. *He saw you and he wants you as much as he wanted us.*

The other two nod.

Well, the cops are on to him. He's not going to get me.

They all laugh, and I scramble off the bed, no longer feeling sorry and heartbroken for them. Something's changed, and I'm not sure what.

He will. He can't be stopped. The middle girl, maybe between sixteen and eighteen, steps toward me. *You'll suffer and die. We can stop that.*

"How?" I ask warily, not bothering to use my internal voice. Stalker dude is long gone.

If you join us, he'll move on, and you won't be in danger.

"Join you?" I don't like the sound of that. "What do you mean?"

Shhhh…

Fingers wrap around my throat, a ghost behind me. How did I not sense her there? I try to claw her hands away, but they're solid and I can't. Her weight presses into me, and the stench of cigarette smoke invades my open mouth. I can't scream, can't speak, can't do anything as her hands get tighter and tighter. My lungs burn from lack of oxygen, and I become lightheaded, unable to stand. As I fall to the ground, black spots start to appear in front of me.

I try to suck in air, but there's nothing but the whine of me trying to breathe. Her fingers dig into my throat, and warmth trickles down my neck.

The three ghosts in front of me are staring solemnly while the fourth chokes the life from me.

My vision starts to narrow, the blackness eating away at the light as my body gives out.

"Ella!"

Eli.

I can't call out to him. I don't have the strength to fight the hands choking me, and my own hands fall to my sides.

There's a loud sound and then the distinct sound of breaking wood.

A gunshot echoes in the room, and the fingers around my throat magically disappear. My lungs are out of air, though.

"Oh, no, you don't, Ella Grace." Eli turns me over, and his lips descend on mine, forcing air into my lungs. Pinpricks of pain stab at them like a thousand tiny needles. "Breathe, Shortcake, breathe for me."

"Ella? What…" Mom rushes over and falls beside me. "What's going on? What happened?"

"Ghost," Eli says and forces more air into my lungs. "Call Ethan. Get an ambulance rolling. I don't want this call on 9-1-1. We can't let the Army know anything in case they're still listening."

He checks my pulse, then starts breathing for me.

His beautiful aqua eyes are the last thing I see before the world goes dark.

CHAPTER SEVEN

"She's coming around."

I hear the words, but I don't. If that even makes sense. It's like I'm in a world full of shades of purple and gray. There are no bright colors, just muted, dark ones. And I'm cold. So very cold. I feel frozen from the inside out. I don't think I've ever felt this cold.

"Come on, Shortcake, open your eyes for me. I need to see those green eyes of yours."

Eli sounds frustrated.

"Please, sweetheart, open your eyes."

Mom sounds desperate.

"Give the girl time. She'll open her eyes when she's good and ready. Not a minute before."

"Gramps is right, Mom. Don't try to rush her. Ella has never been rushed a day in her life. She'll wake up soon enough."

"She's cold," Eli says gruffly. "Cec, can you go ask for more heated blankets? We'll move these and encase her in the warmer ones."

The bed shifts, and then a wave of heat washes over me. He once told me he turned into a furnace for his other charge, Mattie Hathaway, because it's what she needed the most. She'd died so many times, her soul was mostly ghost energy, and her body reflected that through a colder temperature. He said she was always freezing, even when she was standing in one-hundred-degree heat. Did I die and get more ghost energy? It's possible. I remember the ghost choking the life out of me.

Oddly, the thought doesn't scare me. Maybe it's because I'm in this weird, purple hazy world, and I feel safe here. This place reeks of warmth and peace. Like nothing bad could happen here. I know I can't stay, but I really don't want to go and face what put me here either.

It feels so nice, surrounded by warmth and safety. It's hard to get that feeling in my life since being taken by the Army and experimented on. I never feel safe anymore, so this is surreal, which is why I know it can't last.

No, you're right. It can't last.

I look over to see a woman sitting on a rock. Where did that come from? It wasn't here before, but neither was she. I don't know her.

"Who are you?"

"My name is Abagail."

"I don't know you."

"But I know you."

She flips her long blonde hair over her shoulder, and green eyes the same color as mine stare back at me. She looks familiar, but I swear I don't know her.

"Do you know where we are?"

"The waiting room."

That makes no sense. We are not in a waiting room.

"I've been here for a long time. I didn't want to go either because it feels so safe here. I've been waiting for you, Ella. I've often wondered how long it would take you to find your way here."

"I don't understand."

"I know, but you will. Not for a while, but you will. You won't even remember me when you wake up, but eventually, you'll discover who I am, and then we can talk. I've wanted to talk to you for so long. I missed you."

She missed me? Who the heck is this?

"Who are you?"

She stands and comes over to me. "You'll know who I am soon enough, little dove." Leaning down, she kisses me on the forehead. "You have to wake up now, Ella Grace. Be safe. I don't want you here in the waiting room with me. You must live your life and be happy. It's all I want for you."

85

And with that, the world of purples and gray falls away, and my vision is assaulted with bright lights, burning away the memory of the waiting room, as the ghost called it, and her with it.

"There she is," Eli says, palpable relief coating his words.

I blink several times and wince at the light streaming through the windows of my room.

"Close the curtains," I groan. "The sun is like lava burning my eyes."

Cecily hurries to do just that. "Sorry, El. I was trying to keep it bright and warm in here. I didn't want you to wake up to a dark and dingy room."

"My eyes would have preferred dark and dingy, but thank you."

"Do you remember what happened?" Eli asks. "Cecily, go get your mom and Gramps. Let them know she's finally awake."

What happened… I squint, trying to sort through the muddled mess in my head. I have a headache, and it's not helping.

"Not really, but my head hurts. I need Motrin."

Eli reaches over and grabs a water bottle and shakes a few pills into his hand. "Figured you'd want this when you woke up. Cecily said you'd wake up today, so I prepared."

Cecily seems to always know exactly what day I'll wake up whenever I'm unconscious. It's her own unique gift. Gramps says she's a little psychic, but if that's the only thing she can predict, he thinks she's just got a hint of the ability.

"What's the last thing you remember?" Eli hands over the Motrin and the water. "That should help the headache."

"The room at the inn. I woke up and…and there was a ghost there. I think."

"There was. Do you remember texting me and Ethan about the unsub outside your room?"

Unknown subject. He told me that earlier. "No, I don't."

"The guy was trying to break into your room. When I got there, he was gone, but a ghost was choking the life out of you. I had to run and get the shotgun full of rock salt out of the Jeep. I shot her and the others that were just standing there watching her kill you."

"Did you kill them?"

"That's not how you kill a ghost, Shortcake. You have to stab them with a blessed blade, which I didn't have handy, or I would have."

"Why are we here? I thought the door was broken." I glance at my door, which doesn't look damaged at all.

"You've been out for two days, Ella. Gramps had the doors repaired, and we brought you here this morning."

"Two days? Why am I not in the hospital?"

"You were at the hospital. You needed x-rays and a head CT because you were unconscious. You do have a concussion, but not a severe one. Ethan was fretting about not having a secure location since they can't smell the unsub. So this morning, the doctor cleared you to be home to recover since your vitals were good. He didn't want to since you hadn't woken up, but I'll bet your mom is on the phone with him now. He said he'd swing by and check you over to make sure nothing's out of whack."

"Did I die?"

His head snaps up, all his focus centered on me. "Why would you ask that?"

"Because I'm freezing. I've never been this cold in my life, not even when I was lost in the snow in Germany."

He exhales slowly. "You did. You weren't breathing when I got to you, and I gave you CPR until the paramedics got there. It wasn't until they got you to the ER they got your heart started. The CPR kept air and blood flowing so there was no damage to your brain. But yeah, you died for a bit."

"Scared me to death." Mom brushes Eli aside and hugs me tightly. "You have to stop doing this to me, Ella Grace. My heart can't take it."

"Didn't mean to, Mom. I can't control ragey ghosts."

"There was supposed to be a salt line around the property." Gramps comes in and eases himself down on the bed. "I had words with the owners when ghosts got you. They'll be rebuilding their salt wall. How you feeling, girl?"

"Nasty headache, my throat hurts a little, but otherwise not too bad. I'm freezing too. Can't get warm. And I think I have the flu."

"Her body is acclimating itself to having a little more ghost energy than it did."

"A lot more, it feels like."

He frowns and slips in beside me, and a rush of heat blasts out from his body. I literally sigh and snuggle into him. Good Lord, but the boy really can turn into a furnace. He's given off heat before when I was cold, but nothing like this. How can he do this without being a shifter? I guess what he's always telling me is true. He does become exactly what I need him to be. Freaky, really.

"Do you think you could manage some broth?" Mom puts a hand to my head. "At least there's no fever."

"Mama Molly, she got choked, not left out in the snow for hours. She's not gonna get a fever."

"Yes, well, moms always check for fevers, and the ER confirmed the flu. Flu causes fevers."

"My mother does it too." He smiles at her, and Mom's eyes soften. She has quite the soft spot for Eli.

"Now, girl, you remember anythin' about what happened?" Gramps yawns. "Sorry, we ain't slept much the last few days. People breakin' in and attackin' my youngin, then attackin' my youngin again, and then them dagburned inn keepers lyin' to folks about salt lines. It's a wonder we got any sleep a'tall."

Sometimes his mountain speak, as he calls it, is so thick I can barely understand him. Today is one of those days.

"Where's Jamie?"

"He's at his friend's house. He was so worried about you, but I didn't want him here while you were unconscious. I thought after losing both his parents, it might retraumatize him to see you lying so still."

Mom's wringing her hands, which means she's worried she made the wrong decision.

So am I, to be honest. I'm going to get hurt, and he needs to come to terms with that. The only way to do it is to see me hurt and to be here when I wake up. That's the only real way to reassure him.

"Go get him. I'm awake."

Mom nods. "I'll have Emily bring him over. She said she didn't mind, and I don't want to leave you alone."

I'm hardly alone, but I don't say that out loud. She's been through enough without me pointing out the obvious.

"So, any news on the psycho stalker?"

"No. There's been no sign of him since he tried to break into your room at the inn." Eli shifts, pulling me closer, as if he can protect me from even the thoughts of the stalker.

I wish that were possible, too.

"Maybe he left since I'm not easily accessible."

"You think?" Mom perks up, and we all wince.

"No, Mom, I doubt he left. That's not how stalkers work."

"When did you become an expert on them?"

"I am," Eli says before I can get snarky. "My dad hunted more than a few of them. He taught me and my brothers everything he knows about police work and the minds of criminals. Ava too. Stalkers are patient. He'll hunt for months to find her alone. We'll find him first, though."

"Go on and call Jamie. He's probably worried sick."

Mom nods. "I'll bring you back some chicken broth. I made some earlier in case you did wake up."

Ewww, but fine. I'll manage to get some of it down if it makes her feel better.

Once she's gone, Gramps turns serious. "Girl, you sure you're okay? You died on us, and you were dead for a good thirty minutes even though we kept you breathing and your heart beating. That takes a toll on a person whether they want to admit it or not."

"I'm tired, but other than what I described before, I don't think I'm the worse for wear. Tomorrow I might feel different."

He grunts. "We'll see. Tonight, you're safe from stalkers and murderous ghosts alike. You can rest easy, Ella Grace. This is your home, and you're safe here. I promise. I've got people coming tomorrow to shore up security, and Sabien Blackburne is coming to help me redo some of the wards. This place is goin' to be a fortress by the time I'm done."

"I don't want it to be a fortress, Gramps. I want everyone here to feel like it's home and not some fortified prison."

"Don't you worry, girl. It'll feel like home. I'll see to it." He gets up and kisses my forehead. "If I was you, I'd get to sleep afore your mama gets up here with that broth. Don't think I didn't see that grimace. You hate broth."

I laugh. Gramps sees everything.

"Go on, now. Git some sleep."

Eli turns over and pulls me close, tucking my head under his. "He's not wrong. You might experience some residual effects of being dead for so long. Not just physical, but mental. When Dan died, he woke up with a new ability. I'm only telling you this because I know you won't repeat it. He doesn't talk about it to anyone outside of family."

"I won't say a word to anyone, especially not to Dan. I barely see him, though."

"I know, Shortcake. When he woke up, he could pick up an item and see the last few memories of a person who was holding it. Mattie helped him learn to control it, but for a while, he was really freaked out. It didn't manifest until a few days later. So just be on the lookout if you feel or experience anything strange."

Huh. "I'll tell you if something weird happens."

"Good girl." He kisses the top of my head. "You gotta stop dying on me, though. You're going to give me white hair before I'm twenty."

"It would just blend in with all the blond. I think you'll be fine." Yawning, I snuggle closer. "Good night, Eli."

"Good night, Ella."

I close my eyes and drift off into a dreamless sleep.

CHAPTER EIGHT

I'm going to murder Jeff. Why he thought it was a good idea to go camping in the middle of winter, I don't know. Why I agreed to go is a different matter. We've been having problems, and I thought it might be a good idea for us to spend some alone time together away from our friends and family. My parents don't like him, and if they knew I was out here camping instead of at Madison's like I said, I'd be the one murdered.

At least it's not snowing. I've had about all the snow I can handle for one winter. Sure, there's snow on the ground, but it's not supposed to snow more for a day or so, at least. We should be home before the next winter storm blows in.

I sit down beside the little heater we have in the tent. Jeff used the car battery to get power for the heater. I wish he would have done the same for a light, but the heater's glow gives off enough to see by. It's not exactly warm, but it's not freezing either. I have on a thick sweater, and I'm warm enough without needing to put my coat on.

Glancing down, I look at my watch, thankful it's digital and I can see the time. Jeff went to find firewood a while ago and hasn't come back. There's no way he's taking this long to find kindling in the woods. To be fair, there is snow on the ground, and he might be having issues finding dry wood, but he's been gone for about thirty minutes now. I'm all for just bypassing the fire and staying in the tent. Body heat is better, anyway.

But Jeff wanted the fire. He said it would help to keep wild animals away too, as if I didn't know that growing up here in the mountains. The idea makes no sense, really. It's cold. You'd think the wild animals would be drawn to a heat source. I would if I were out here all night in the snow and the cold. But he's right. Wild animals do shy away from fire. I don't know why.

Getting up, I unzip the tent and look outside, hoping to see him, but all I see are the shadowy trees in the darkness. We're camped in an area where the trees are thick overhead, and even though the branches are bare of leaves, it's hard for the moonlight to breach the patchwork of the barren canopy overhead.

A burst of wind slaps me in the face, and I quickly zip the tent back up before too much cold air gets in and chases out what little heat I have. I'm actually starting to worry about Jeff. He knows these mountains as well as I do, but he might have run into a starving animal or a mama bear who woke up from her hibernation unexpectedly. He could be out there hurt or bleeding.

Part of me wants to go look for him. Finding his tracks in the snow would be easy enough, but I also don't want to confront starving animals. Which is why I should have said no to the camping trip.

He'd come find me, though.

Growling in irritation, I put on my puffer jacket, grab the flashlight, and go brave the cold. The wind is harsh, blowing right into my face. It's nights like this you need a ski mask despite the damage to your hair. My daddy always says better warm than glam. He's not wrong, but it is what it is since I don't have one currently.

Turning on the light, I sweep it over the ground and find his tracks in the snow easily enough. They lead deeper into the woods at the base of the mountain. Of course they do. He couldn't stay in and around camp looking, could he? Jeff loves to make things difficult in the name of doing everything right. He's a stickler for perfection, which is where our problems come into play. I'm a hot mess most days, and I don't care if every single thing is perfect. If I didn't love the big lug, I'd have broken up with him months ago.

"Jeff?" I call, hoping he'll hear me and come back. Not likely over the wind whistling around me, but I try anyway. Putting my head down, I start to follow his tracks, calling out every few minutes.

I walk along, growing more and more worried. I'm going to have to find service and call my daddy. He's going to be mad, but if Jeff is lost out here, maybe hurt, he needs help. Daddy will call in everybody he knows and get the deputies up here to find him.

"Jeff? This isn't funny. If you're hurt, just call out. Please!"

Silence.

The shadows are deeper here as well. Small patches of moonlight filter through every few yards, but not enough to matter. The wind is loud against the silence surrounding me. Why is it so quiet? I swear it's my own imagination freaking me out. I watch way too many horror movies.

"Jeff, yell if you can hear me!" I stand still and listen, straining to hear over the howling of the wind. My flashlight follows his tracks deeper into the woods, and I sigh, forcing my feet to keep walking despite the hinky feeling I have. He's out here somewhere, probably hurt. I'm not leaving him. I'll look for ten more minutes, and then I'll backtrack to the camp and try to find a signal to call Daddy.

I'm just about to call it quits when my flashlight falls on something peculiar. Another set of prints starts to follow Jeff's. My hinky feeling gets stronger, but I ignore it. Did someone see him get hurt? Are they trying to help him?

Going closer, I notice the tracks are about the same size and definitely male. It's the same kind of track my dad's work boots leave in the snow. They came out of the trees to the right and start to trail Jeff's. Maybe whoever it is noticed the shoe prints and decided to make sure no one needed help?

It's times like this I wish I was a shifter so I could just smell what's going on. My mother is human, and my dad is a witch. I inherited none of his abilities. So I'm about as human as you can get. I have no way of vetting the situation, which makes me even more worried for Jeff. It might not be some good Samaritan trying to help. I mean who would be out here in the dead of night except for teenage idiots?

Growling in frustration, I start to follow both prints. After five minutes, I notice they start to get sporadic and all over the place. It's almost like Jeff is running and the second set of prints is calmly walking. Maybe he did just find Jeff's prints and is trying to help him.

I start to doubt myself a minute later when the tracks disappear. I take several steps and then stop, my heart dropping into the pit of my stomach. There, against a tree, is Jeff. His head is down, but I recognize his jacket. There's a trail of blood leading from where I'm standing to the tree.

"Jeff!" I run to him but stop again when I'm a hair's breadth from him. He has blood on him. It's soaking the entire front of his coat.

"Jeff?" I whisper and reach out to touch him. He's cold, but I push his head up. Dead eyes stare at me, and I glance down to see his throat slit from one side to the other, the blood now frozen instead of gushing.

I scream and turn to run back to camp, digging into my coat pocket for my phone while trying to keep a firm grip on the flashlight. Panic eats away at my thoughts, but I do my best to push them down. Daddy taught me to keep my head no matter how scared I am. Telling and doing are completely different things, I realize. Fear pushes me on, but it doesn't help me forget Jeff was murdered and the killer is still out here, probably watching me.

That thought drives my legs to run faster, and soon, I'm back at camp. Diving into the tent to get the keys to Jeff's Dodge truck, I let out a scream of frustration when I remember he put them in his pocket when we *got here. I'm not going back there to search for them. I know where we left the truck. My cousin taught me how to hotwire a car. The truck is older and should be about the same as an old model car when it comes to this.*

Deep breaths, I tell myself. Calm down. Hard to do, though, when every other image is Jeff, staring up at me, his throat cut.

Shaking my head to try to clear my thoughts, I turn to go back out when I see a man standing in the opening to the tent. He's tall, his hair blending in with the dark hoodie he's wearing. That's all I can really tell about him because it's dark.

"Hello, Chelsea."

He knows my name? How does he know my name? Why does he know my name?

"Sorry about Jeff. He'd just get in the way of our fun."

Oh, God. He killed Jeff.

"Nothing to say? The others always ask who I am and other stupid questions I'm not going to answer. I like that you're not playing that game. It won't help you or make things easier, though. I like to play rough."

Others?

"Come along, sweetheart. We have a long way to go, and I want to get out of here before anyone notices you're gone."

I shake my head. Nope, nope, nope. I'm not going anywhere with him.

"No."

He cocks his head. "No?"

"No. You killed Jeff. You'll just kill me."

"I will kill you, but not for a while. We have games to play first. I really don't want to hurt you before we get home. Blood is a pain to get out of the seats in the truck."

I glance around and grab the big walking stick Jeff brought in earlier in case we needed one. It's a strong, sturdy stick. I may not be a shifter, but I am the captain of the softball team for a reason. I can handle a bat like nobody else. A stick will do in a pinch.

"Feisty. That's what I like about you. The others were very submissive. You're my test case for Ella. She'll be a handful, and I need to alter my plans for that."

Ella? I don't know who that is, but I hope to God he never gets his hands on her. I

106

can't worry about her right now, though. I need to get out of this tent, and he's blocking my only exit.

As if reading my thoughts, he steps away. "Go ahead, Chelsea. Run. I like it when they run. It'll be so much sweeter when I catch you."

Now, I understand what it actually means to be a deer in the headlights, unsure of what to do and where to go. Does he really mean it? He'll let me run?

He sweeps his hand out. "Go. I'm not going to stop you. I'll even give you a head start since you spent so much time looking for Jeff and I simply walked back here and waited on you. I'm rested. So you deserve those few precious moments to try to get away."

If I stay, it's impossible, but I have a chance if I run. I'm just not sure he'll actually let me. In the end, a chance is better than doing nothing, and I carefully slip around him, clutching my stick, ready to strike if he moves so much as an inch.

Then I run.

I've camped and hiked in these woods all my life, but in the middle of the night, running for my life, with the terrain covered in snow, it looks different. It feels different. Sinister, almost, with the deep shadows and the howling wind trying to push me down at every turn. It's like the woods are working against me.

I turn in the general direction of the truck and see our tracks from earlier. Thank God for the snow. But at the same time, I'm leaving a clear trail for the murderer to follow me. I can't think about that right now. My goal is to get to the truck.

The wind fights me. I can't hear if the guy is following closely or not. Which makes my own fear and anxiety ratchet up a notch.

Five minutes later, the woods open up a bit, and with it, our tracks from earlier disappear. The wind has washed them away. Which way? The environment looks completely different, and I can't remember which way we came. But I can't stop. I pick a direction and go, hoping I chose right.

It's not long before my sides start to burn and my breathing becomes labored. I've been running for so long. Athlete or not, a person can only go so far on pure adrenaline. If I stop, I die, and I know that, so I push through the pain and the burn that's now in my lungs.

I should have seen the truck by now. I picked the wrong way, and I slow down, trying to figure out where I am. I know I can't rest long, but I need to stop for a minute. Breathing hard, I look around, hoping to make sense of my surroundings, but for as long as I've lived in this area, I'm lost. That sends me reeling more than anything else. I don't know where I am.

Twigs snap close to me, and I start running again. Might have been an animal, or it might have been him. I'm not standing around to find out.

I'm turned around, and I veer left and start to double back, hoping I can skirt around the guy chasing me by sticking to the trees and the shadows.

"Chelsea, I see you."

He sounds like he's whispering in my ear, which makes no sense. He'd have to be right beside me for me to hear him over all this wind. I stop and turn completely around, looking for him, but all I see is the trees and the snow.

"I'm right here." Fingers sweep over my cheek, and I scream, trying to run. I can't see him, but how is he touching me?

I zigzag through the trees, running until my legs give out and I fall, tumbling down the path. My back comes to rest against a tree, and I gasp for air, doing everything I can to force my body to move, but it's too worn out.

"There, there, little one. Everything's going to be fine. You tried your best, but now it's time to give up."

My gaze sweeps the area. Where is he?

He's behind me.

He squats by my head and runs his fingers through my hair.

"I love the color red. Before the night is out, you'll be covered in it."

Not this girl.

As he steps in front of me, I focus every last ounce of energy I have and kick at exactly the right moment. My foot connects with his genitals, and he drops to the ground screaming.

I waste no time and get up, staggering as my legs try to give out, but I'm an athlete. I'm trained to fight through the pain.

It's not long before I'm jerked backward, and I scream in sheer rage. The fear is only enhanced by the fury.

"You shouldn't have done that, Chelsea. Now I have to hurt you." He pulls me around, and as I'm about to kick him again, his fist comes down, and the last thing I see are his eyes. One's blue and one's brown.

It's the only clear thing about him, but it's enough to follow me into my nightmares as the world around me goes dark and I know I'm as dead as Jeff is.

Only my death won't be as quick.

CHAPTER NINE

It takes everything I have not to scream when I wake up in a cold sweat, my heart beating out of my chest, and unable to catch to my breath. My hand goes to my eye where the girl in my dream was hit. It's sore.

"Hey, hey." Eli's right there. "You're fine. Everything's fine."

He went to sleep on the floor in my room. He's spent so many nights there because of my nightmares. I appreciate him more than I can ever tell him.

"Sorry," I mutter and reach over to turn on the light.

"Never be sorry for things you can't control," he says firmly, glancing at the clock. "At least you slept through the night this time."

There were a couple of weeks where I might have gotten an hour of sleep at best. It was back when I couldn't remember what happened to me when the Army kidnapped me. Those nightmares were worse than when I got my memory back simply because I couldn't understand what my mind had hidden from me and what it was trying to show me at the same time.

"This isn't like that," I say softly. "I think I saw what happened to one of the girls. It was like it was me it was happening to, though."

Eli curses. It's not often he does.

"What?"

"I think more of your abilities are waking up since you've got so much more ghost energy now."

"What kind of abilities?"

"You've seen some things before, so I assumed you had a psychic or a Seer in your heritage somewhere, but I've looked. You don't."

"Okay?"

"The problem is there's not a lot known about living reapers. There've been so few of them throughout history, there's very little we do know. Hilda could do what you just described. We had to give her a tattoo to keep her from physically and emotionally experiencing a ghost's death. She was there in the memory as if she were the person, which sounds like what happened to you. She felt what they felt."

I nod. "Exactly. I woke up, shaking, barely able to catch my breath. My eye is sore where he hit her."

Another curse slips out of him.

"We assumed it was because she had a Seer in her family history, but since you don't, I think it's a natural ability a living reaper grows into as they gain more ghost energy in their soul."

"This is a bad thing?"

114

"Depends."

"On?"

"Do you think you can handle experiencing every death of every ghost who comes to you?"

"That sounds unpleasant."

"It is, and I'm afraid if we don't do something to dampen this now, you'll have the same experience Mattie did."

"Which was?"

"A girl was raped, and she felt every moment of it."

"Yeah, no. I got the feeling that was what was going to happen to this ghost, but she fell unconscious, and I woke up. I don't want that."

He takes a shaky breath. "There's an issue with the tattoo."

"Yeah?"

"The one Caleb gave her, it wouldn't have worked. Silas had to fix it."

"Silas…the demon who gave me back my memories?"

He nods. "I don't want him anywhere near you."

"He seemed nice enough."

"Never let him hear you say that." His fists clench in rage. "He'll use it against you. He's a demon, Ella Grace. It's his job to convince you he's harmless, then he'll trap you in a deal that steals your soul. It's who he is. You can't trust him. Ever. Do you understand me?"

"If you don't trust him, then I'll trust your judgement."

He really didn't seem all that dangerous to me. Charming, sure. He even seemed like he wanted to help me.

"How does a tattoo stop this, anyway?"

"It's not the tattoo, exactly. It's the spelled ink that does the heavy lifting. The tattoo design is part of the spell that guides the ink into what it's supposed to do."

"Good luck convincing Mom to let me get a tattoo. She and Dad were adamant about Cecily and me never getting a tattoo."

"When she understands what it'll do, she'll agree."

She will. I'm not even sure she'll pitch a fit once she understands how it'll protect me. She might, though. Mom's hardcore against tattoos.

"So, if this tattoo is hard to do without Silas' help, how do we do it?"

"I'll figure it out. I need to call Hilda anyway to see if her dad has ever run up against a Supe with no scent. I don't want to call Dad, but I will if I have to."

If he ends up doing that, his father will come here. Then the game will be up, and everyone will know who he is, where he came from, and that he used to hunt Supes with his family. Eli has changed since coming here. He doesn't hunt anything and everything that moves. He still hunts here and there, sure, but it's the rogue Supes, and ghosts who have gone demented from being here too long. He considers himself a Supe now.

I saw what happened when Jordan found out about his past. I don't want him to lose the place he considers his home. I won't let him. Even if I have to call and threaten his father with mine. I'm willing to bet my dad has more juice than his, and I'll call Major

Henry Banks to protect Eli the way he's protected me.

"What say I call Hilda and upset my brother about waking him up before dawn?"

"That's mean."

"That's what little brothers are for." Eli grins devilishly and fishes for his phone in his makeshift bed. "Ready?"

"We should wait. It's only five-thirty."

"It'll be fine." He finds the contact in his phone and puts it on speakerphone.

A very deep, growly voice answers the phone. "This had better be an emergency. I just went to sleep an hour ago."

"Oh, Dan, sorry. I meant to call Hilda." The twinkle in his eyes belies that statement as well as the grin on his face.

"No." Dan's voice gets deeper. "She's been really sick with her pregnancy. Squirt's puked so much she's lost like ten pounds in two weeks."

Eli winces. "Sorry. I didn't know."

I can imagine his brother shrugging. "What do you want, little brother? I'm tired."

"We have a situation."

"Situation?" His voice is instantly alert. Eli's brother is a detective in the New Orleans Police Department's supernatural division.

"I can't call Dad. He'd come here, and it would blow my cover, and I don't want the residents to feel threatened. You and I both know Dad would look at everything to find a reason to invade. He doesn't differentiate between a good Supe and a bad one."

"I had hoped getting to know Jason and his family would mellow that a little."

"Me too, but if he could find a way to remove Jason from Ava's life without causing her pain, he'd do it. Some days I think he'd do it anyway if Mom wasn't putting her foot down."

"If he ever does, the Blackburnes will murder him."

I don't doubt that.

"So, you see why I don't want him here?"

"Yes, now explain what's going on."

Eli spends the next ten minutes telling him all the events of the last few days and the unsub's history.

"James is going to get wind of this, and when he does, he will go there."

"I know, which is part of the reason I want to get this solved quickly. I was hoping Hilda could ask her dad if he knows of any Supe who doesn't carry a scent."

"I wonder…"

"What?"

"You remember the last thing Mattie went up against? The child-creature the Army created?"

"You're thinking they might have created this thing and turned it loose?"

"Maybe. I'll check with Zeke and let you know. How fast do you need this information? I've only been asleep for an hour. If it can't wait, I'll drag myself out of bed and find out."

"No, you get some sleep," I cut in before Eli tells him to go find out now.

"Oh, Ella, I didn't know you were there. Sorry about what happened. Sounds like you're as scrappy as my girl."

"I'm not stupid. I've seen enough horror movies and read enough books to know trapping yourself in an obvious place is a bad thing to do."

"Squirt is a diehard horror movie fan too. She says the only thing that can scare her is her own imagination working overtime."

"That and walking upon a ghost who died horribly."

"That too," Dan says ruefully.

"Speaking of, there's something else I need to talk to you and Hilda about."

"She really hates that nickname."

"I know. Why do you think I still use it?"

He sighs. "What else do you need information on?"

"You remember that spelled tattoo Caleb inked Hilda with? The one that kept her from experiencing a ghost's death?"

"The one Silas declared was wrong and he had to fix?"

"Yup."

"Yeah, what about it?"

"Ella died twice since the last time you saw her and has gained some abilities. One of which is ghosts being able to show her their deaths."

"You're feeling the deaths?" Dan asks, his voice slightly sharp in alarm.

"I woke up this morning from a dream feeling everything she felt, including where the killer hit her in the eye before she blacked out. That's why I woke up, because she passed out."

Dan starts cussing. "I know for a fact the ink Caleb gave Mattie wouldn't have worked. I may not personally trust Silas, but when it comes to Mattie's safety, I trust no one like I do that demon. I trust him as much as I do Zeke when it comes to her. When the demon found out she was expecting, he went into overprotective mode, going so far as warding Zeke's place with wards no one has seen in centuries. Do you want me to ask him to ink Ella?"

"Not if it's going to cost anyone anything. We don't make deals with demons."

"No, we don't," Dan agrees. "If he won't help, I'll call Caleb and have him study Mattie's. I'm not sure if he can replicate it. It's very complex with twists and turns and incantations at every crosspoint."

"I'd appreciate it," I say, since it's for me.

"Those visions can be very emotionally harmful." Dan moves, and we hear a mattress squeak. "Shh, no, go back to sleep, sweetheart." Someone murmurs something. "No, it's not work. It's Eli asking a question. I'll tell you about it when we both wake up later."

It's quiet for a minute, and then a door opens and closes.

Eli grimaces, looking upset that he woke up his sister-in-law. The same woman he loved with all his heart when he was alive, but she loved his brother. That was a recipe for pain and disaster. He thinks it was a blessing he died when he did because she would have had to choose, and that would have destroyed him, her, and his brother. I have to agree. Plus, it brought him here, and he's a part of our family now. As much as it sucked for him to lose his family, he also gained one that gave him so much more freedom than he had as part of the Malone clan. His future was predetermined by his father, and now his future is open to him.

"Sorry, had to step out of the room. We woke her up. She should go back to sleep, as she's exhausted. I think after this one, she's not going to want another one."

"Dad always said the same thing, according to Mom, and she had three."

"My dad said the same thing, and we got Cecily."

He sighs. "She's miserable."

"Her body is changing to accommodate a tiny person. Once she gets through the first trimester, it should get better."

Eli quirks a brow at me.

What? I paid attention in health and biology class. It's not weird I know that. And besides, I'm a girl. It's natural for us to be curious about pregnancy. If more boys were, maybe there wouldn't be so many teenage parents.

"God, I hope so." Dan sighs heavily. "I'll catch a couple hours of sleep and then talk to Zeke. I've never heard of a Supernatural who doesn't have a unique scent. Zeke might at least know who to call to get information about it. Is there anything you can tell me about him?"

I describe for Dan exactly what I did for Ethan. "And one more thing. In my dream, he had one brown eye and one blue eye. That should make it easier to track him down."

"You'd think, but most criminals who are good at what they do will realize that is a unique and identifiable trait. He might be savvy enough to put in contacts when he's around the normies."

"The normies?"

"It's what Pierce calls humans."

"Who?" Eli and I both ask.

"Evan Pierce. A half demon who is friends with Mattie. I've spent so much time around him the last couple of months, I've picked up some of his slang."

"Wait, isn't he the guy who had the hots for Hilda?"

"The same, but he and I came to an understanding."

"You beat him down?"

"No, didn't have to. He understands I'll put him down if he makes a single move on her."

"Smart man."

"Back to this stalker serial killer of yours. Heterochromia is an unusual trait. It may play a factor in whatever condition or ability he has that allows him not to have a scent. It's a good lead. I just hate how you came by it. I'll get on that tattoo first, though. Caleb may insist on coming to ink you."

"No," Eli and I say together.

Dan goes quiet.

"We don't want Dad here. It'll blow my cover. You know it will, Dan."

"Yeah, I know, little brother. I'll figure something out." He yawns. "I have to sleep. I've been up for forty-eight hours with less than three hours of sleep."

"Go on and sleep. We're up for the day, but I get you need to rest. Getting old sucks, doesn't it?"

"Do you want a beating, Elijah?"

He laughs. "Goodnight, Dan." He hangs up the phone before Dan can respond.

"Why are you so mean?"

"It's a little brother's job. I told you that. Come on. Let's go make coffee. I doubt either of us is going back to sleep. We can hit the Hathaway Foundation's database with this new trait and see what we can find."

"Sure. You start the coffee. I need to pee."

"Didn't need to hear that, Ella."

"Tough."

He sticks his tongue out at me and jumps up, making a beeline for the door.

He's such an idiot sometimes, but he made me laugh, for which I'm grateful. I needed to laugh after that dream. We'll call Ethan later and update him, I'm sure.

Throwing the covers back, I get up and go to the bathroom. Maybe I'll take a shower too. I feel like I need to wash the stink of fear off me. I can still feel her emotions, and a hot shower might be the best medicine for me.

Plan in hand, I gather up some clean clothes before heading to the bathroom. God knows what the day is going to hold. A shower will help me get ready to face it.

At least I hope so.

CHAPTER TEN

The day wore on with no movement on what kind of person or creature didn't have a trackable scent. It made no sense to anyone we spoke to. Gramps called all his contacts, and no one had any idea of what he was describing. It wasn't until there was a knock on the door around suppertime that we got some answers.

"You expecting someone?" Eli asks as Gramps meanders over to the front door.

"Nope." He looks through the window and stops. Just stands still.

"Who is it?" Eli goes over and looks as confused as his grandfather.

"Uh, guys?" Cecily and Mom come in carrying platters of food.

Eli shakes himself and goes to answer the door, but Gramps stops him. "I don't know if I want that man in my house."

"It's fine, Gramps. Zeke wouldn't be here if he didn't know how to help."

"He's dangerous."

"Yes, he is, but he considers me family, and he's not dangerous to his family."

Who are they talking about?

When Eli opens the door, a very tall man steps in. His shoulder-length brown hair is windswept, and his blue eyes are sharp as they take in the room. He reminds me a lot of that actor on Fox's *Sleepy Hollow*. He just looks like someone who should be in the colonial era.

"Hey, Zeke."

"Eli." He smiles warmly. His voice is very cultured and very southern with a French lilt to it. "As soon as Daniel told me what you had here, I was on the first flight out of New Orleans."

"You've seen it?"

He nods. "I've tracked it for well over ten years."

"You can track it, then?" I ask, relieved.

"Not in the sense you are thinking, *ma petite âme*. I've been able to track its kills, but it moves on well before I get there. It's been disheartening, and I'd begun to think I'd never get the upper hand."

Ma petite âme? What does that mean?

"Introduce me to your family, Elijah. We must remember our manners. I told your mother I would ensure you are remembering them."

"Sorry," he mutters, looking chastised. Any mention of one's mother and the word manners tends to do that to us all. "This is Ella, her sister, Cecily, her mother Molly Banks, and of course my grandfather, Marco McGreggor. Everyone, this is Hilda's father, Ezekiel Crane."

"*Enchanté*," he says, eyes sparkling.

131

"I don't think anyone speaks French, Zeke."

"Nonsense. Marco speaks it perfectly well. I simply said it's a pleasure to meet you all even if it is under such grave circumstances."

"That one word does not mean all that."

"*Non*, Ella, it does not. It means 'delighted,' which we French translate to 'delighted to meet you.'"

That's cool. I like it. I may use it from now on. *Enchanté*. It'll drive Gramps and Eli nuts.

"Mr. Crane." My mother puts the serving dish on the dining table and rushes over. "I've wanted to thank you in person for so long for everything you did for Ella and getting the Army out of our town. We can all breathe a little easier because of it."

"You are more than welcome, *Madame* Banks. I was happy to help. Elijah is a part of my family, and since you are his, you are all now a part of my family and under my protection. I understand why Marco may not appreciate it, given my reputation, but I assure you, it's a good thing."

"He's right," Eli chimes in. "It will make people more wary when thinking of coming after Ella again."

"Except for the psycho stalker serial killer intent on murdering me."

Zeke, as Eli calls him, frowns. "Daniel explained everything that happened. I am so sorry, Ella. It had to be very traumatic for you."

I shrug. I've gone through worse. So has my sister, for that matter. Given what this guy has done to his victims, I may not have felt the same if he'd gotten his hands on me.

And I'm still relatively calm about it all, aside from in the moment it was happening. I'm not panicked or freaked out. Being calm is what's freaking me out. Not sure why I'm reacting this way. The normal thing would be to stress, to cry, to be scared all the time. I'm scared, yeah, but not overly so.

"Ella?" Zeke cocks his head. "What's wrong?"

"Nothing. Just thinking."

He frowns like he doesn't believe me.

"I have a daughter who's very much like you. I know when she's not telling the entire truth, as I suspect you are not."

"Now, see here," Gramps starts, but I cut him off.

"It's fine, Gramps. I was just thinking about how calm I am in spite of the guy stalking me. That's all. It's weird. Mr. Crane was right. I guess I think the way I'm feeling is wrong."

Zeke nods like he understands while everyone else stares at me, confused. See, this is why I didn't say anything. I don't want them to be worried.

"Given everything that you've been through since your move to Jacob's Fork, the way you're reacting is perfectly natural. It will take a great deal more than a stalker intent on murder to scare you. You should chat with *ma petite* sometime about that. Or you can talk with me. I understand it completely."

"Thank you."

"Would you like to stay for supper, Mr. Crane?" Mom asks, lifting the heavy mood somewhat. "We were just about to sit down."

"Oh, I wouldn't want to intrude…"

"You will never be intruding in my home. You and your daughter helped save my daughter's life. Eat with us, please. It's nothing fancy, just fried chicken, but Eli loves it."

Zeke grins. "Fried chicken is one of my favorite things, only eclipsed by homemade mac and cheese."

"We have that too. My youngest, Jamie, loves it."

"Please call me Zeke. It's what my friends and family do. And I would be honored to share a meal in your home. It will give me a chance to tell you about what I know."

"Not in front of Jamie. He's been through enough real horror without hearing about more."

"The child you adopted?"

Mom nods. "He comes from a very abusive home, and we do our best to not talk

135

about anything he might consider scary in front of him. Ella has even refrained from her horror movie marathons when he's home."

"My daughter has a love of horror movies as well. I completely understand and will respect your wishes. We can discuss the Chameleon after supper."

"Is that what it is?" I ask.

"That's the name I gave it since it seems to take on all the traits of a real chameleon. It may have a proper name, but this is what it is to me."

Gramps looks thoughtful. "I need to check the database with this new information."

"Not until after supper." Mom gives him her best Mom stare, and he looks down. No one can withstand that stare.

"After dinner," he agrees.

My mom made really good fried chicken before, but one of the ladies she met at the library where she volunteers gave her a different recipe. She didn't follow it exactly, but she changed hers based on that recipe, and I swear, she'd win every competition she enters with it. She taught it to me too.

It takes a few minutes to finish getting food on the table and to add another plate. Gramps looks about as happy as a soured grape at the prospect of having dinner with Ezekiel Crane. I'm not sure why. Eli's spoken of him before, and I got the feeling he didn't trust him very much, but he seems to have changed his opinion on that. I'll get him to spill once Mr. Crane leaves.

It doesn't take long for Jamie to start asking a million questions once he knows our guest is from New Orleans. The accent makes my little brother grin from ear to ear as he tries to mimic it. Mr. Crane took to Jamie like a duck to water. Before dinner's over, they're thick as thieves. Gramps appears alarmed, while Mom's just indulgent.

"How's Nancy doing?" Eli asks after a bit.

"Very pregnant and unhappy I came here when she's so close to delivering, but it's important."

"Pregnant? What are you having?" Mom perks up at the idea of a new baby. She always wished she had more kids, but Dad said two was enough since he was gone so much.

"We don't know. The little one is shy whenever we do an ultrasound. Nancy laughs, and I'm disgruntled. I refuse to paint the nursery some bland color like she wants me to. As soon as we know what we're having, I'll get the painters on it. We've picked out the colors for both a boy and girl."

"And if you don't find out before the baby's born?"

"Then he or she will sleep in our room until the nursery's finished."

"How many children do you have, Zeke?" Mom pushes her plate away from her, content to chit chat.

"I have a son and daughter and the one on the way."

"I know Emma is in her twenties, but what about your son?"

"He's a year older than Emma Rose."

"I bet they were a handful growing up."

He gets this pained look on his face. "I didn't get to see either of them grow up. Emma was taken from us when she was two, and we didn't find her until she was seventeen. Cass's mother never told me I was his father. We only found out last year. It's been hard getting him to trust me."

"I'm so sorry. I didn't know."

"No reason you should." He smiles, but some of the happiness is gone from his eyes. "He and I are working on our relationship, and the one I have with my daughter is rock solid. With both of us showing Cass I am no danger to my family, I'm sure he'll come around."

"Why would he think you were a danger to him?" Cecily asks, speaking up for the first time.

Zeke glances at Jamie, who's more involved with finishing his dinner than anything we're saying. Or at least that's what it looks like. We all know kids take in a lot more information than we think they do.

"How about we table that discussion until later?"

Cecily opens her mouth, but Mom is faster.

"That sounds perfect. Do you have room for dessert, Mr…er…Zeke?"

His eyes warm up again. "I'm a sugar fiend."

Mom laughs. "I made a blackberry cobbler."

"I grew up on peach cobbler, but I've never had a blackberry one before."

"Marco has a small horde of blackberry bushes here on the property. We canned more than I can possibly use in a year, so we use the berries in a lot of desserts."

"Blackberry dumplings are better," Jaimie pipes in, and I knew I was right. He *was* listening closer than it appeared.

"Really? What's the difference?" Mr. Crane asks, fascinated.

"One's baked and one's made in a pot, like chicken 'n dumplings. Mama makes 'em both good."

The entire table, except for Mr. Crane, freezes. It's the first time he called Mom anything except Molly.

She clears her throat. "Thank you, Jamie."

He grins, his teeth full of chicken.

"Gross, Jamie." Cecily pretends to gag. "You have chicken in your teeth."

He laughs and starts running his tongue over them. "Mmmm, good."

"Jamie, mind your manners. We have a guest." Mom's disapproving tone gets his attention immediately.

"Sorry."

"No worries, little one. But your mother is right. Manners are what set you apart from others. It's a testament to how you were raised, and from everything I've seen, your mama is raising you right. You want to make her proud of you, *oui*?"

Jamie nods solemnly.

"Then mind your manners. Now, let's try this blackberry cobbler, and then I suppose it's a bath and bedtime for you."

He sighs. "I don't like baths."

Mr. Crane laughs. "Neither did I. I used to hide in the garden to try to escape mine when I was your age."

"Did it work?"

"No." It's Mr. Crane's turn to be disgruntled. "My mama had x-ray vision. She always found me no matter how well hidden I was."

Jamie grins, and it's not long before dessert is served, of which I get a separate non-sugary version. I have to suffice with the natural sugar of the berries, which isn't as much as you'd think. Still, it's very good. Cecily hates it, but I've never tried the sugared version, so I have no comparison.

Once everyone has finished, Eli and I clear the table and load the dishwasher.

Jamie's gone to get his bath, and now we might get some actual answers.

I'm not sure whether it's a good thing or a bad thing.

I guess we'll see.

CHAPTER ELEVEN

Ethan arrives as Eli and I finish loading the dishwasher. I'm surprised. Gramps must have called him. He sniffs the minute he enters, and a snarl curls his lips. It has to be Mr. Crane he's smelling. Mom's cooking never brings on that reaction.

"Hey, Ethan." Eli closes the door behind him. "Gramps call you?"

He nods, his brown eyes hunting the room. "Where's Crane?"

"In the study with Gramps. They're looking through the database or updating it

143

or something. Zeke claims to know what's hunting Ella."

I really don't like that visual. The thought of being hunted is unnerving.

"Keep that man away from Molly."

"Why?" Cecily asks. "He's done nothing but help us."

"Ezekiel Crane is a very bad man."

"How?"

"He's a criminal who has never spent more than an hour in an interrogation room because he's good at being a criminal. He makes deals with demons, and everyone in the supernatural world knows his name and to steer clear of him."

"It appears my bad PR has even followed me here." Mr. Crane smiles sardonically. "I am a man who has done bad things, and I admit to nothing. But I'm also a man who loves my family, and Eli is a part of that family. He considers Ella family, so her entire family by extension is part of mine, and I make sure my family is safe. In this instance, Sheriff, you have nothing to fear from me and everything to gain."

"Look," I butt in before anything else can spew out of Ethan's mouth. "He's here to help with the stalker, and he's been nothing but nice to my family. Until he does something that causes me not to trust him, I'm going to trust him. So, can we put away the testosterone and get down to what's important? Finding this Chameleon before he finds me?"

Ethan looks like he swallowed yesterday's liver and onions, but he pipes down.

"Good. Now, let's go before Jamie wonders what all the noise is." I wave toward the hallway, and we all follow Mr. Crane back to Gramps' office. Except for Cecily. She goes upstairs to help Mom. Jamie insists on Cecily reading him his bedtime story every night. She enjoys it as much as he does.

He looks up when we come in. "I'm updating the database now with all the information Crane has given us. It seems like there're a lot of entries that appear random, but I think it's all the same creature.

I'm pooling them now under the new name, Chameleon. Crane's been tracking it for years."

Ethan's eyes sweep to Mr. Crane. "You know how to track it?"

He shakes his head. "I know how to track its kills. As I was explaining before, I am never in the town he's hunting in. I only come after the carnage."

"How did you come across him?" I ask and sit down on Gramps' comfy couch.

"He killed my cousin."

I wave toward the other end of the couch since it's the comfiest seating in the room. "Can you tell us?"

He nods and sits. I see the slight grimace before he erases it. You'd never have seen it if you hadn't been looking. I bet his couches are a hundred times more comfortable. He has that air of having the nicest things money can buy, but at the same time he doesn't come off snobby or entitled.

"Emily Rose was my mother's niece. She was more of a sister to me than a cousin. We grew up together, and she mostly stayed with us since her parents traveled so much. I even named my own daughter after her. That's how much she meant to me. Emily was full of life and laughter. She saw the good in everyone. She kept me sane when we lost Emma Rose. I remember that first day when I came home. Mama called her because I just sat there in the nursery unable to move or speak. She managed to snap me out of it."

I can't imagine what losing a child would do to a person. Just thinking of someone doing something to Jamie or Cecily upsets me to the point of a nervous breakdown.

Zeke sighs heavily and pulls himself from his memories. "We were in Providence doing a deal with a manufacturing outlet. The town was excited because it was going to bring a few thousand jobs to the area. Emily loved to help people, and she fought hard to bring the opportunity to the town. She had a mind for business unlike any I've seen outside of my son's. She was a beautiful, kind soul, and I will see justice served in her name."

He looks off into space, and I imagine he's seeing her in his mind's eye, or some memory they shared. He looks so sad and hurt underneath all the anger.

"We had just signed all the paperwork and went out to the local bar with some of the townspeople to celebrate. She met a man there. He was tall, dark hair, but I remember his eyes. They were mismatched. One blue and one brown. He gave me a bad vibe, but Emily only laughed when I told her. She said everyone gave me a bad vibe when it came to protecting her. To which I informed her I'd drag her out of the bar kicking and screaming if she even thought of going anywhere with him. She laughed, but she stayed in the bar. Later that night, we both returned to our hotel, and I said goodnight."

Ethan finally sits as the story pauses. His demeanor has softened as he listens to Mr. Crane. You can hear how much he loved his cousin as he talks about her. There's no doubting that. I dread what's coming, knowing this story doesn't have a happy ending.

"The next morning, she didn't show up at breakfast, and I went to find her. She wasn't in her room. I checked with the front desk, but they hadn't seen her either. I started calling around, hoping she was somewhere with one of our new partners, engrossed in plans, but no one had seen her. She couldn't be located, so I called the police. They came and began to search. They found her phone in the dumpster behind the hotel. Three days later, her body showed up on the front steps of our hotel. She'd been beaten, tortured, and raped. And disfigured."

"What color was her hair?" I ask, a knot forming in my stomach.

"Red."

Sounds like my stalker, but something's bothering me.

"My stalker didn't look old enough to have killed your cousin. He'd have aged enough that I would have seen the difference."

"I would agree except for this creature's unique ability. He can change his appearance and take on the form of another.

149

As I said, the only thing he can't change is the color of his eyes. Let me get my briefcase out of the car. I have drawings of the different forms he took while in towns where his victims lived."

"How did you get those?"

"The police, of course." He stands and leaves the room.

Ethan sighs heavily. "This is not a good idea, inviting that man here."

"No one invited him," Gramps grumps. "He showed up."

"I called Dan, and Dan talked to Zeke, who jumped on the first flight." Eli shrugs. "I didn't used to trust him either, but since I've gotten to know him, I do. He won't do anything to harm anyone in this house. He will protect them with his life."

Ethan doesn't agree, but it's a moot point. Mr. Crane is here now, and if he can help us catch this guy, then I'm all for him staying.

Mom comes and stops when she sees Ethan. "Oh, Ethan. I didn't know you were here. I was giving Jamie a bath. Cecily's getting him ready for bed. Have you eaten?"

She says it all in a rush. Yeah, she's definitely getting ideas from our discussion earlier. She sounds almost girly. It's rather disturbing coming from my mother.

"No, no, I haven't. Did I smell fried chicken?"

Mom nods. "I'll go make you a plate."

She turns and leaves the room. Ethan looks away from the now-empty doorway when Gramps clears his throat.

"Don't."

The one word is low, deep, and deadly, and a tone I've never heard come from Gramps before.

"That woman has been hurt enough without dealing with you finding a mate bond later…"

"She *is* my mate," Ethan interrupts and leaves Gramps stunned.

"Your expression is exactly how we felt when he told us," I say, not even able to laugh. I'm worried about this.

"She ain't ready."

"I know. It's why I'm just her friend right now."

Gramps nods. "Make sure it stays that way."

Mr. Crane comes back carrying a large leather briefcase that looks super expensive. He goes straight to the desk and opens it, pulling out file folders until he finds what he's looking for. Opening it, he spreads out over a dozen drawings across Gramps' desk. The images are varied and not at all alike.

"The police were able to determine the presence of the person in these sketches in the lives of the victims. Sometimes they were caught on camera, sometimes someone saw them. Either way, composites were drawn. I'm not sure I believe they are one hundred percent accurate, but I believe they give us an idea."

"Which is what?" I get up to study them. "They don't look like each other at all."

"No, they don't, which is why tracking this creature has been so difficult," he agrees. "But there is a similarity." He flips the pages over and there are handwritten notes on the back. "He always chooses dark hair, and his build is similar in all his shapes.

In every surveillance tape I watched, he wears similar clothing. A dark hoodie, jeans, and white sneakers. As you can see, all the notes dictate the same."

"So, you want us to look for every man in town with dark hair wearing a dark hoodie, jeans, and white sneakers?" I raise an eyebrow. "Don't think that'll work, as a lot people wear that. We're a college town, and that's pretty standard for most of us around that age."

"No, of course not. You'll be looking for the one with the mismatched eyes."

"Can't he just put in contacts?"

Zeke finally smiles, and it is predatory. "No. It's his one disadvantage. Contacts don't work for him."

"How do you know this?"

"I spoke with someone who knows more about him than I do." He digs around in his briefcase and comes up with a large journal. "I took notes."

"Who did you speak with?"

"Do you really want to know, Sheriff?"

Ethan swallows. "Probably not."

"He only has one weak point, then?" I pull the focus of the conversation to the discussion at hand. Best not to dwell on Mr. Crane's unsavory contacts. It'll only make Ethan mad.

"Yes. If you want to take him down, you have to disable his eyes. If he can't see, he can't change."

"Pepper spray?"

"If only," Mr. Crane mutters. "*Non, ma petite âme*. You have to…" He frowns, unsure how to say what he wants to say.

"You have to shoot them out or gouge them out or something, right?" Eli takes pity on him. "Something so he can't get his vision back?"

Mr. Crane nods. "*Oui*, Elijah. However, getting that close to him will prove very dangerous. He's been at this for a very long time, and he's good at it."

"How long?"

He opens his journal and flips through it. "According to this, there are five living Chameleons. The oldest one is almost a thousand years old. This particular one is almost as old, his age somewhere close to nine hundred or so."

"According to your source," Ethan says slowly.

"Yes."

"I want to know who the source is."

"He is someone who knows them well. I can't tell you more than that. It would violate a deal I made."

"He wouldn't tell you how to track him?"

"It's not that he wouldn't tell me. It's that he didn't know how."

"If you made a deal. Does that mean the information came from a demon?" I ask.

He smiles. "You are very perceptive, *ma petite âme*."

"What does that mean?"

"It means 'little soul.' You are a keeper of souls, so that is what I call you."

Huh. I like it.

"So, what do we do now?"

"Now we set a trap and wait."

"Trap?"

"He's going to come for you, Ella. It's not in his nature to let his prey get away. We'll be waiting when he does."

I'm not sure I like the sound of this. I'm not up to being bait.

"You are *not* using my youngin' as bait." Gramps stands to his full height, and I see the Angel in him for the first time. That glorious bluish-white light that shines off Eli starts to shimmer around Gramps, and I can literally feel his Grace shining out of him.

"I hadn't considered it." Mr. Crane stares him down, neither flinching nor backing down. "Our children must be protected at all costs, and I'd never put Ella in danger for any reason."

"Then what did you mean?"

"I meant he's coming for her. We can't do anything about that. It's in his nature to finish what he starts. I have that as gospel from my source. I think we use that. We set traps around Ella so we can catch him before he gets close to her. No one is going to leave her side until we catch him. We use his own drive against him. That's what I meant."

"Knock, knock." Mom sounds strained. I bet she heard all that. She has a plate in one hand and a glass of iced tea in the other. "Everything okay in here?"

"Just dandy," Gramps says with a growl.

Mom looks to me, and I nod. "Just a difference of opinion. You know how men can get when they are trying to make a plan."

Mom tries to smile but doesn't quite manage it.

"Thank you, Molly." Ethan takes the plate from her, concerned she heard what we were discussing too. I can see it on his face. "Ella's right. Everything's fine."

"You're sure?"

He nods. "Trust me."

"Oddly, I do. I need to check on Jamie. Let me know if anyone needs anything."

Once we're sure she's gone, Mr. Crane turns to me. "I promise I would never put you in danger. There are so few of us living reapers around, and we need to stick together and protect each other."

"You're a living reaper?" Why did I not know this? Why didn't Eli tell me?

"Yes, but it's not something people outside of my family know, so I am trusting all the people in this room to keep that quiet."

Gramps grunts. "Didn't know that."

"As I said, I keep it close to the vest."

"You have to be a very holy person to receive that gift." Gramps' shrewd gaze narrows in on him. "How did you manage that with all the things you've done?"

Zeke's smile is dark. "I'm a good man who has done bad things. If the Powers That Be recognize that, then I say let it alone. I answer only to my maker and no one else."

Huh. I don't count myself as holy. I'm not sure I even believe in organized religion. There's Rhea, but I can see and touch her. I've spoken with her. She's done what she promised. But even then, I'm not so sure about the whole religion thing.

"We're off target," Eli says, yawning. "Can we borrow your journal and go through it tonight, Zeke? We can get together tomorrow and come up with a plan of action."

"Of course, Elijah." He hands the book to Eli. "I'm also here about the other issue."

"Other issue?" Gramps frowns. "What issue?"

"Daniel said Ella is in need of a specific spelled tattoo to keep the ghosts from forcing her to relive their deaths. Did you die recently, *ma petite âme*?"

"Why do you ask?"

"It would be the only way you would have gained that ability."

I nod. "A ghost tried to strangle me to death. I wasn't breathing when Eli got to me."

Zeke strokes his chin thoughtfully. "It will be interesting to see how your abilities develop. I've looked into your bloodline, and there are no Supernatural relatives I could find. We will need to be careful of letting you die more. The human body is not meant to house the abilities of a reaper, and the more you die, the more abilities you will gain. That is what happened to my daughter and myself. Those abilities could cause health problems."

"The headaches," Eli mutters darkly.

"Yes. Emma Rose is a bit more protected, and she's unique in her heritage, so she could take more than most. Keep an eye on Ella, Elijah. If she starts to get headaches, call me. I'll have Emma's neurologist on the first flight out."

This ability can hurt me? Great. Just great.

"About the tattoo?" I ask instead of asking more about Eli's worried look. I'll deal with all that later. Focus on the problem at hand.

"The only one who can ink it correctly is Silas. He did mine and *ma petite's*. It's very intricate and the spells are so complicated, I wouldn't even trust the Blackburnes to do it."

"But you trust a demon to do it?" I ask softly.

"In this? Implicitly."

"We are not making deals with a demon," Gramps announces. "He'll want something."

"Yes, he did want something, and I made the deal for Ella. She'll have no repercussions from him."

"Why would you do that?" He doesn't even know me.

"Because it's important, and I hold more markers against Silas than he does against me. I am able to organize deals with him that bring no harm to me and mine because of it."

I'm not sure how I feel about him making a deal with a demon to give me a tattoo.

"The experiences will only get worse, Ella Grace. To the point they could drive you mad. You won't know what's real and what's a memory of a ghost. I've experienced it firsthand, and I can tell you, it's unpleasant. It's painful when you get overwhelmed. The headache it causes is debilitating. Silas will give you all the same protections Emma Rose has against the ghosts so they can't overwhelm you, and they won't be able to force you to experience their deaths. There will be no debts owed to the demon on your part."

I glance over at Gramps, who looks like a skunk just sprayed him.

"You sure he won't want nuthin' from my youngin'?"

"I'm sure, Marco. She needs this to stay sane. You know that better than I, since you were the one who helped me as a child when it became too much for me. If I recall, you introduced Silas to me."

What?

Everyone stares at Gramps.

"Fine, have the demon come tomorrow to ink her."

Zeke nods. "The Blackburnes have graciously offered to have me to stay with them. That is where I'll be should you need me before tomorrow morning."

"Uh, I'll be at school."

"Uh, no, you won't," Eli gently rebukes. "You're sick."

Zeke glances at me. "I did notice you had a flushed face. Are you ill?"

"I have the flu."

Everyone who's not a shifter backs up.

"The ER doctors gave me medicine, which I'm taking religiously."

"As long as you have a fever, you're contagious." Mr. Crane packs up his briefcase. "I'll call before I come over in the morning. I don't want to wake anyone up too early."

"Thank you, Mr. Crane."

"Call me Zeke, Ella Grace. Everyone who matters to me does. Before I go home, and after we catch this Chameleon, you and I will sit down and have a chat about all things living reaper. Any questions you have, I will do my best to answer or find the answer to. You have a teacher?"

"Yeah, she's actually pretty good about the teaching part."

"I'm glad they are doing right by you, but if they don't, let me know. I will make sure your education doesn't suffer because of a Reaper unwilling to teach you."

The velvety threat of the dark rolls over his tongue, and I shiver. For the first time since he walked in the door, I'm a little afraid of him. He said he was a good man who did bad things. But even good men go bad when they do enough bad things. How close is he to becoming a bad man who does bad things?

We all say our goodbyes, agreeing to meet at breakfast.

Gramps throws us out, telling us we can read the journal tomorrow.

Eli shrugs and tells me to go to bed and get some rest. I look rough, apparently. And flushed.

Taking some Motrin, I actually do go to bed.

Hopefully, there will be no more dreams tonight.

CHAPTER TWELVE

I woke in the middle of the night with the strangest sensation. It wasn't fear, it wasn't trepidation, but it was something. Uneasiness, maybe. I'm not sure. One thing I do know is I'm safe from ghosts here. Gramps has an impenetrable salt line around the borders of his property and another one around the house about a hundred feet under all the pipes and cables necessary for modern amenities.

Maybe it's just all the talk of the Chameleon from earlier. I don't know.

Either way, I'm not going to be able to go back to sleep. I know my body well enough to understand when I can and can't sleep. Plus, I feel like crap. I'm pretty sure my fever's back, as my whole body feels hot to the touch. My throat is sore, my nose is running, and I ache all over. Never get the flu if you can help it. That's what my grandmother always says. She's right. The flu sucks.

Going downstairs, I flip on the kitchen light and find a cold bottle of water in the fridge and down it in one go. I'm dying of thirst. Has to be the fever. Grabbing another bottle of cold water, I turn off the kitchen light and go flop down on the couch and cover myself with the giant fuzzy throw Mom picked up at Kohl's. As hot as I feel, I'm also freezing. Sure signs of a fever. The Motrin is upstairs in the hallway bathroom, but I'm too tired to get it. I just want to lie here and suffer in peace.

Which lasts all of five minutes. Cecily comes down the stairs, flipping on lights as she goes.

"Gah, my eyes!"

She quickly turns off the overhead light in the living room but leaves the staircase light on.

"I thought I heard something," she explains. "It was you, I guess."

I nod and pull the throw tighter around me.

"You don't look so good, Ella."

"Fever."

"Did you take some Motrin?"

I shake my head. "It's upstairs. I'm too tired to go back up and get it."

"I'll get it for you." She turns around and returns within a minute or two carrying the giant-sized bottle of Motrin. Shaking a few out, she hands them to me before plopping down beside me.

"Careful, or you'll get sick too."

"Nope. I had the flu shot."

"Didn't I?"

"Uh, I think you were unconscious in the hospital when I had mine."

"Which time?"

She smiles wryly. "Can't remember."

"Find something to watch if you're not going back to bed. All this silence is bothering me. I've gotten used to a lot of noise since Jamie came to live with us."

"Yeah, I know what you mean. I was here alone last week, and the place was so silent I turned on the TV and cranked it up really loud just for the noise."

She flips through a few channels before switching to Paramount Plus. "Want to watch *1923*? It's prequel to *Yellowstone*."

"Didn't we already watch that?"

"No, that was *1883* with Tim McGraw and Faith Hill. It was how the family got to their homestead. This is the next generation set in 1923 with Harrison Ford."

"Ah." *Yellowstone* is a family favorite. Even Gramps enjoyed it. We were all sad when it was canceled after season five. There was so much more they could have done with the storyline. But at least we get these spin-off shows.

She goes over to the closet and pulls out a few more throws, tossing two of them over me, before she settles down. Her long blonde hair is in some kind of intricate braid she needs to teach me how to do. My sister is the spitting image of our mother with her blonde hair, blue eyes, and near-Amazonian height. I'm the short one, like our dad. Oddly enough, her height has never stopped me from being the big sister, ready throw down when someone hurts her feelings. She's kind and easily hurt by the words of others. I've thrown a few punches when someone made her cry, much to Mom's horror.

"Are you okay? I mean aside from feeling like death from the flu."

"Yeah, just tired. I don't even have the bruises from being choked anymore. Eli's healing abilities are getting better."

"Eli said you didn't remember it."

"I don't, but that doesn't mean my brain doesn't. I jump at things for no reason, and I have to wonder if it's because of what I went through. Or if it was because of my dream last night. The mind is weird, you know?"

She nods. "I've been thinking."

"Never a good thing." I start hacking up a lung when I laugh.

"Serves you right," she grouches, but I see the smile hiding beneath the surface of her ire. "Seriously, though. I've been thinking a lot about going into psychology."

"Really? Why?"

"You."

"Me?"

"When you lost your memory, it got me thinking about why you couldn't remember, and I talked to my therapist about it. She explained that when a person goes through so much, their mind will shield them when they go beyond their breaking point. I want to study that and find ways to help people not only cope with it, but perhaps regain their memories through treatment. The human mind fascinates me."

Wow. I didn't know my memory loss had such a profound impact on Cecily. As hard as that experience was for me, it's nice something productive came out of it.

Talking about the human mind is probably a good time to talk to her about

Leo. Or my fever-fogged mind thinks so, anyway.

"Cec, there's something I wanted to talk to you about for a while, but I've been hesitant."

"Why? You know you can talk to me about anything."

"It's about you."

"Me? Then you definitely can talk to me about anything."

"You might get mad and so pissed you don't want to talk to me again."

She shakes her head and grins. "Nope, never happen. I almost lost you, and that feeling beats anything else."

"Ditto."

We've both been through that. Me when the Army took me for experimentation, and her when her boyfriend kidnapped her and held her hostage. It was the wolves who found her. She'd escaped him and gotten lost in the woods. It was Cole Walker who found her. Leo's Alpha.

"Do you remember me telling you what a mate bond is?"

"That's for the shifters, right? It's when they find the person meant for them. It doesn't matter how much they might love the person they're with. When they find their mate, they drop them and focus only on the mate. It's sweet in a way, but awful too. Especially for the person who gets dumped."

I nod. "Yeah."

"What's that got to do with me?"

"Leo."

She cocks her head curiously. "Cole Walker's friend? The big one who always seems so intense?"

"That would be him. You're his mate."

She sucks in a breath and looks at me like I've lost my mind. "That's not possible."

"It's true. Remember when Cole gave us a ride to the diner after that one football game? Leo was there first, and he finally got close enough to you to scent you. Your scent hit him like a ton of bricks, and he almost shifted there in the stands in response. They had to take him away before he did. That's how powerful a mate bond is."

She says nothing.

"Cole came to the house that night to talk to me and Eli. You remember that?"

She nods.

"It was about Leo and what to do. You're not old enough to date him. And you're still recovering from everything that happened. That night, you flinched away from him when he got to close. None of us thought you were ready to know this. I wanted you to have a normal life. I wanted you to be able to heal, to fall in love with someone, to have a natural high school experience without this overshadowing everything. I've wondered for so long if not telling you was a mistake, but I was so worried."

"Why tell me now?"

"I've had the chance to see what a mate bond really means by getting to know Jason Reed and his mate, Ava. Even Cole and his mate, Clementine. I've watched how close they are, how their every need is a priority. I've heard you can't deny a mate bond because it's so strong, and I didn't understand that statement until I watched them. They're close, like one being that no one can separate. Knowing someone could love and protect you like that…maybe keeping you away from that knowledge is doing more harm than good. I watch you flinch whenever a man who's not Jordan, Eli, or Gramps gets near you. Maybe knowing Leo would cut off his own arm before hurting you or allowing someone to hurt you might help you. And he's your mate. You deserve to know that. I've worried for months that I was wrong to keep it from you, but my only goal was to protect you. I'm sorry."

"Wow." She pulls her legs up and wraps her arms around them, hugging them to her chest. "That's a lot."

"I was thinking about Jordan, too. You really like him, and he likes you. I thought you two deserved a chance. He's been really good to you."

"Didn't you just say you can't walk away from a mate bond?"

"That's what everyone says, even though they say in the same breath there's a choice.

It's different for a human, and they can choose to walk away. I don't know. You could talk to Ava, maybe. She's human. She could tell you if it's a possibility to say no."

"It doesn't seem fair, does it? To fall in love and then have that ripped from you over a bond you didn't choose."

"No, but from what I've observed, the bond is amazingly beautiful, which is why I thought you should know. There's someone out there meant specifically for you who will love you, cherish you, and protect you with every fiber of his being. Even if you don't choose him, there is no other choice for him. He'll always look out for you. You may not even know it, but he'll keep you safe for as long as you live. As I said, there is no other choice for a shifter. They mate for life."

"It's all so sad. What if he was in love with someone before this mate bond thingy activated?"

"I don't know. I don't know him that well. It's something to ask about, maybe. You've got a couple of years before you're even old enough to think about him."

"How old is he?"

"I dunno. In his early twenties, I think? I'm pretty sure he's a junior in college, and he, Cole, and Jackson are planning to try for the NFL."

"I have years to make any kind of decision, then."

"Yeah. Are you mad?"

"I don't think I am, but I'm not sure what I'm feeling. It's a lot to take in."

"I thought you'd be mad at me. So mad you'd never speak to me again."

She lets out a laugh. "No, Ella. You're my sister, and that matters more to me than any boy. Mate or not, you'll always be my sister. Remember what Dad taught us?"

"You grow up, you get married. Spouses come and go, either through death or divorce. Kids grow up and get married. Parents die. All you're left with is your siblings. Keep them close and remember, when everyone else is gone, they're who's left."

"Exactly. That's why you and I will always be good, even when we're so mad we can't stand each other."

I really thought she'd be spitting mad. It is crazy that she's not. I kept a very big secret from her, and she's letting it go. I hope if she keeps something like this from me in the future, I can think back and remember this conversation and be as grown up and mature as Cecily is right now.

"What are you initial thoughts about Leo?"

"Shock. I don't know him except that he's Cole's friend. I see him around a lot more than I used to."

"Yeah, he keeps eyes on you to make sure you're safe. I have noticed you pay more attention to him than you used to."

"What do you mean?"

"When he's in the same room, you watch him. Your eyes will always find him, and you shift a little closer to where he is."

"I really do that?"

"Yes. I think it's the mate bond. Even when you didn't know about it, you did. That's another reason I decided to tell you."

"Huh." She stares at the TV, not really seeing the show playing. "I didn't realize. I've caught myself staring a few times when he's around. I mean he is cute, but he's so big."

"Uh, sister mine, you're an Amazon yourself."

"I don't mean his height. Still, even at my height, the boy is taller than me. What I meant was his mass. He's huge."

"He's a wide receiver, Cec. Of course he's huge."

"I know, but…El, have you looked at him? It makes me feel vulnerable. He could seriously hurt me if he chose."

"He'd never hurt you. I know that much about a mate bond. He'd throw himself in front of a train to keep you safe."

"Are you sure?"

"Yeah. I've learned a lot about it since I found out he was yours. I trust no one like I do him when it comes to you."

"But you don't know him."

"But I know the bond and what that means to a shifter."

"Maybe," she mutters.

"You think it might be worth having a conversation with Ava about?"

"Maybe."

"It's a lot. Why don't we restart the episode and forget about it tonight?"

"Sounds like a plan." She uncurls her legs and pulls the throw back up on her lap. "Do you think Ava would talk to me about something so personal?"

"I'll have Eli talk to her. Can't hurt to ask."

"No, it can't hurt to ask. Thanks for telling me."

"So, do we have anyone cute in this one?"

"The nephew is supposed to be gorgeous, but we'll see if he's drool worthy."

She restarts the episode, and we both settle down, neither of us really watching the show. Her thoughts are lost with the bomb I just dumped on her, and mine are still fuzzy from the fever.

It's not long before my eyes droop, and the noise of the TV fades to give way to sleep.

CHAPTER THIRTEEN

The cabin sits alone, and the longer I stare at it, the more I want to run and hide, only my feet are frozen in place. Why am I here again? I don't want to be here. I want to be anywhere but here with all those graves in the back yard. It feels like the ghosts back there want to hurt me. I might be wrong, but pain, I understand.

They don't want to hurt you. It's been a while since anyone could see or hear us. They just want to leave, but we're tied to him. We can't leave.

181

The woman leaning against the tree startles me with her voice, but she doesn't scare me. Her dress sweeps the ground, and the deep green color matches her eyes perfectly. Her hair is done up in some kind of fancy style I've never seen before. An emerald necklace graces her throat.

"Who are you?"

My name is Dorothy Graham. Who are you?

"I'm Ella. Why are you all here?"

She points to the cabin. Because of him. He holds something dear to us, and it won't allow us to leave.

"I can help you to move on if you want."

She smiles sadly. Others have tried, and his hold on us is too strong.

"Who is he?"

The devil.

"I don't believe in the devil. Just bad people who do bad things."

She laughs harshly. You'll change your mind if he collects you to hold here with us, forever to relive the nightmare he put you through.

That would be awful.
"Where is here?"

I don't know. I was there, and now I'm here.

"Where are you from?"

Albany, New York.

"What year is it where you're from?"

She looks at me as if I've asked her a crazy question.

It's 1867.

That explains the dress and the hairstyle.
"Where I'm from, it's 2025."

Her pale face goes even paler.

I've been here that long? That cannot be right.

I nod. "It is right. I can help you, though. I'm what's called a living reaper. I can see and hear the dead. My whole job is to help you be able to move on to the next life."

You think everyone here is dead?

"Yes."

She shakes her head. We can't be. I would know if I was dead.

"Has anyone else been able to see you?"

Only the others, but no one comes here. His home is well hidden.

"Do you remember when you met him?"

Yes, I was at my father's home. Edward was there to do business. My father was a merchant, and Edward had wares he'd brought from overseas to show to him. Mother was very put off by him. It was his eyes that disturbed her. One was blue and one was brown. They fascinated me, and he was very charming.

I'm not sure I'd call him charming, but her initial experience with him was far different from mine.

I saw him on and off several more times over the next few weeks. He came into my father's store in town, and I always saw him then as well. I had hoped he might be taken with me. His stories of adventures in faraway lands gave me so many hours of daydreams. I wanted to go on these grand adventures with him. To experience the wilds of Africa. See the lions and feel the sun on my face. Dance in the rain in the streets of London. I was a smitten fool.

She's young, maybe a few years older than me, and he took advantage of that. He charmed a very naive young woman to gain her trust, only to kill her later. It's cruel.

Every time I saw him, I felt like I knew him and he knew me. The feeling became stronger as the weeks passed. Then it came time for him to go on his travels again, and I was devastated. He hadn't asked my father anything to do with me. One night, he woke me up. He was in my room, and I don't know how he'd gotten in there. I locked my room from the inside at night. He asked me to run away with him. He told me he had asked my father for my hand, but Father told him no. That his daughter would marry someone wealthier than a common trader. I, of course, was outraged. It didn't take long for me to agree, and I quickly dressed, packed a small bag, and we snuck out of the house to the horse he had waiting. We boarded his ship that night.

Women were so much more naive back in the day.

The ship's captain married us that night.

185

Oh, he married her?

But it wasn't long before his true colors came out. He started to beat me when I disagreed with him. There were days I never left our cabin because of the bruises. When we reached the Caribbean, I thought things would get better. But they didn't. He took me to his home, and the servants were as afraid of him as I'd come to be. There was no help for me there.

The poor girl. I'd thought of her as a woman when I first saw her, but the more she talks, the more I realize she's more of a child than Cecily is. My heart breaks for her.

Then the worst of it came. I understood who he truly was. He brought home a young woman, bound and gagged. He took her to the rooms below. I could hear her scream, but I was afraid to go down there. He'd come up for dinner covered in blood and looking satisfied. One day, when he'd gone into town, I got up the courage to go downstairs. My thought was to release her so she could get away, but what I saw...it made me crazed. He'd dismembered her.

There were parts of her scattered everywhere. He'd mounted her head on the wall, along with several others. All of them young women with red hair. I ran, screaming, back upstairs, but the stairs were slick with blood, and I slipped. I fell and hit my head. That's the last thing I remember until I woke up here.

She fell and hit her head. That's when she died, and she doesn't know it. How to convince her she's dead, though? There's no one else around who can't hear her.

She sucks in a breath, and I look up, alarmed. The lights in the cabin are on.

He's home. I must go before he notices I'm gone. Don't go near the cabin. If he sees you, he'll want you, and I have no power to stop him.

The young woman disappears and reappears next to the door. It opens a moment later, and a man steps out of the cabin. I shrink into the tree, trying my best to hide, and hope he doesn't see me.

He's dressed in jeans and a hoodie, but he's not looking at me or Dorothy. He's looking at something he's holding. I'm not sure what it is.

Dorothy wrings her hands much as my mother does and says something, but the man doesn't look up or even acknowledge her. I tilt my head, watching closely. I don't think he's ignoring her. He can't hear her. He growls, and Dorothy flinches, but it's not directed at her. It's directed at the object in his hands. What is it?

Inching closer, I try to get a better look, but it's no good. His back is to me, and there's no way to see what he's holding unless I want to get really close to him.

A twig snaps when my shoe crushes it, and his head whips up. I go as still as possible as he searches the trees surrounding the cabin.

Please don't see me. Please don't see me.

He steps off the porch, searching the tree line.

Run, the scratchy voice from the last time I was here screams into my ear.

I don't wait; I turn and run in the opposite direction of the cabin, staying in the trees and hoping he doesn't catch up to me. I do not want to go in that cabin.

It's not long before I hear him behind me. He's faster than I am. Dodging around trees, I try to make it harder for him to get me. Running in a straight line is sure to have him catch up to me faster. He has to see me by this point, but I don't dare turn around. Instead, I try to run faster.

I blame it on the snow. I didn't see the tree root rising out of the ground because there is such a thick layer of snow. My foot catches it, and I trip, falling to the ground, my knees hitting hard.

It takes only a moment for me to get up, but that's all he needs to catch me. Fingers grip my arm, and he turns me around. Those bi-colored eyes gleam with glee when he sees who he's caught.

"Ella Grace. What are you doing here?"

Before I can answer, I'm sucked out of the dream, and I sit up in my room, barely able to catch my breath.

This is not good.

Getting up, I go looking for Eli and Gramps.

CHAPTER FOURTEEN

Before I can wake anyone up, there's a knock at the door, bringing with it a whole new set of problems. Problems that make me forget my dream. Ones no one expected. Zeke stands on our front porch with a pale face, a piece of paper clutched in his hand.

"Ella, where is your grandfather?"

"He's not downstairs yet."

"Please go get him. Urgently." He comes inside, closes and locks the door.

I glance at the paper but turn and go upstairs to pound on Gramps' door.

"Girl, it's too early for all this noise."

"Mr. Crane is here, and he looks very upset. He has a piece of paper he's holding on to for dear life."

He frowns but picks up his hat and shoves it on his head. "Let's go see what all the fuss is about, then."

"This was taped to your door." Mr. Crane hands the note over to Gramps as soon as he sees him. Gramps reads the paper, and his own face loses its color as well.

"What is it?" This reaction is starting to scare even me.

"Let's wait until your mother takes Jamie to school."

"I do not think letting anyone out of this house is a wise course of action." Mr. Crane puts his briefcase down. "Has your sister left for school?"

"Jordan was supposed to pick her up. I just woke up."

"Aye, I saw your sister get in Jordan's truck out of my window earlier." Gramps takes a deep breath. He does it only when he gets really worried and tries to settle himself. It's a habit of his.

"Elijah!" Mr. Crane calls, and Eli comes running down the stairs. There was a definite note of alarm in Mr. Crane's voice.

"What's wrong?"

"Go fetch Cecily from school. Marco, can you call and let them know he's coming and she's to come home without delay?"

Gramps nods and pulls out his phone, walking a short distance away.

"What does the note say?" I ask.

"It spoke of how beautiful you and your sister looked while you slept last night, curled up on the couch like twin angels waiting to be defiled."

He keeps his voice low, but I can't contain my gasp of outrage. Talk about me all he wants, but keep his grubby, rapist thoughts and hands off my baby sister. I'll kill him before I let him near her.

Better yet, I'll call in the secret weapon. One I know will protect her with his life.

Going to the table and picking up my phone, I call Leo. He picks up on the first ring.

"Hello?" He sounds sleepy. Football season's over, so maybe he slept in.

"It's Ella. You need to come over here right now."

"Is something wrong? Is Cecily okay?"

"Better yet, can you meet Eli at the high school and come home with them both?"

"Of course, but…"

"Do you know what happened to me the other day?"

"Your house was broken into, and the intruder was looking for you."

"Try serial killer rapist, and now he's talking about Cecily. Had the gall to leave a note on our door describing us as angels waiting to be defiled."

The snarl that comes through the phone is enough to raise the hair on Mr. Crane's head. His expression turns startled.

"I'll get right there. Make sure Eli knows I'm coming. I'll follow them in my truck to keep from scaring her."

"I told her who you are. She needs some time, but I think she'll talk to you about it eventually."

"You told her?" His usually strong voice is unsure. "Was that wise?"

"Yes. I think it'll help her heal in the long run. Now, please hurry. This guy can't be tracked. Shifters can't smell him, so keep alert."

He asked no more questions, just hung up.

"I heard you," Eli says before I can say anything. "It's a good call."

"Who was that?" Mr. Crane asks when Eli leaves.

"Cecily's mate. She's too young for him to do anything about it, but he'll keep her safe. I trust him like no one else."

"A mate bond is one of the strongest forces in supernatural nature. He'll die to keep her safe. I could ask for no better protection for your sister."

"Your sister? What happened?" Mom demands as she rushes over, Jamie behind her.

"Seems the intruder left a note on the door describing me and Cecily as we were sleeping on the couch last night. Eli went to get Cecily. Leo's meeting them at the school."

"Who?" Mom frowns, trying to place the name.

"He's one of Cole Walker's betas."

"One of his seconds in command?"

"Yes."

"Why send for him?"

"He's Cecily's mate, and right now, I trust him to protect her more than anyone else." I state it matter-of-factly, but Mom is floored.

"She's too young! That boy is in college."

"Yes, he's well aware of that and respects it. It doesn't negate that he will protect her better than anyone else."

"She's right, Molly." Mr. Crane comes over to stand by me. "A mate bond is stronger than anything else in this world, except perhaps the love a parent has for a child. Some would argue it's stronger than that, but I don't know. Leo will give his life to protect your daughter."

"I don't like this." Mom starts wringing her hands. "After everything she's been through…"

"Leo's aware, and he will go out of his way to make her feel comfortable even if it means staying outside in the cold to keep his distance. Don't worry, Mom."

"Don't worry, she says," Mom mutters. "One child almost killed, now the same man is making threats against both my girls. Telling me not to worry is like telling me not breathe."

"Mama?" Jamie's voice interrupts us all. "Is someone bad trying to hurt Ella and Cecily?" His big brown eyes are terrified.

"Oh, baby, it's okay. No one is going to hurt them. I won't let them." Mom rushes over and gathers him to her. "No one is going to hurt you or the girls. I promise."

I shouldn't have said anything with Jamie in the room. I was just so upset at the thought of this creep going after my sister I didn't think.

"Jamie, how do you feel about skipping school today?" I go over to him and Mom and sink to my knees. "You and I can play any game you want. I bet I can even beat you on that racing game you like."

"No school?" He frowns.

"Me and Cecily are skipping school too. I think it'll be fun. We can make your favorite lunch, and I might even talk Mom into making some of her homemade peanut butter fudge. What do you say?"

"Is it because of the bad man trying to hurt you?"

There is no glossing anything over with this kid. "Yes, but that doesn't mean we can't have fun, does it?"

He disentangles himself from Mom and throws himself at me. "Don't get hurt, Ella. Please don't leave me."

I hug him as tightly as I can. "No one's taking me away from you. I'm safe. You're safe. And Cecily is safe."

"Promise?"

"I promise." I hope it's a promise I can keep.

"Okay," he whispers.

"Go on upstairs with Mom and put your pajamas back on. We'll do a PJ day. I'll put mine on too. What do you think?"

"Can we watch *Paw Patrol*?"

"Anything you want, kiddo."

"And you'll stay here where the bad man can't get you?"

"Promise."

"Okay." He hugs me so hard I swear he's going to cut off access to air before he lets go. "Stay here. Don't go anywhere until I come back down."

"Sure, kiddo."

He frowns but runs back upstairs. Poor kid. He's still very insecure after living with abusive parents and then living with the fear that we might one day not want him. We do our best to reassure him daily, but it's a fear he may always carry with him.

Jamie comes back quickly, his eyes wild and searching for me. It's not until they settle on me that some of his panic dissipates.

"How about breakfast? You hungry?"

He nods.

"Chocolate chip pancakes? I bet Mom will make some."

"With chocolate syrup?"

"I think we can con Mom into that." He giggles, but the worry doesn't leave his eyes. "Come on, shorty, let's go find us some food."

All talk of the stalker is cut short because, right now, it's about Jamie. Everything else can wait until we get him settled.

I was right. Mom agreed to make him chocolate chip pancakes with chocolate syrup without so much as a blink of the eye. Me? I made eggs with whole grain toast. As much as I'd love to indulge in the sugary sweetness everyone else will be eating, I can't. Diabetes sucks on the best of days, but when there are yummy pancakes around, it sucks harder.

Eli, Cecily, and Leo come in while Mom is plating up the last of the giant stacks of pancakes. Ethan is on their heels. She looks at them, then at the food, and sighs. Putting everything back in the warmer, she starts to make more.

I, too, make more food. Shifters eat a lot. So does Eli, for that matter. We're going to need twice as much as we made.

Leo starts when he sees Mr. Crane. His eyes narrow, and he moves closer to Cecily, but other than that, he has no outward reaction. It's obvious he knows who he is, but he at least has manners and is keeping his thoughts to himself. Good man.

"I need to see…"

Mom cuts Ethan off with a look and nods toward Jamie, who is engrossed in a game on my phone, sitting at the table. No more talk of the note and who wrote it. We don't want him any more upset than he is.

Ethan catches on and glances at the kid. Jamie is tiny for his age due to malnourishment and abuse. He doesn't look gaunt anymore, and he's filled out quite a bit since getting regular meals, but he's still small. The doctor thinks he should hit a growth spurt soon, but so far, he hasn't. His dark hair and even darker eyes are a stark contrast to his pale face this morning. He's unsure and shaky, like he was when he first came home to live with us. I hate it.

"I hope everyone is hungry." Mom starts pouring more pancake batter onto the hot griddle. She bought the extra-large one at Walmart over Christmas. At least she has an excuse to use it now.

"Mom, this is Leo Cooper. Leo, this is my mother, Molly Banks."

"Ma'am." Leo tips his head toward her, his eyes studying everyone and everything.

"You know everyone except for Mr. Crane, I think." I gesture toward Mr. Crane with my spatula. "He came to offer his help."

Leo nods toward him.

"Are you always this quiet?" Cecily asks.

"Yes."

Well, then.

She does not look impressed, but I am. He dropped everything to make sure she's safe, and that's all that matters to me.

"Marco, should the children wait in the panic room, do you think?" Mom asks thoughtfully.

We all cringe at the word *children*, even Leo.

"It's not a bad idea, especially with this 'un in there with 'em. He's not going to let anything near 'em."

He's in his mountain speak today, which is sometimes unintelligible.

"We will need Ella and Eli upstairs, however." Mr. Crane folds the paper he'd been reading. "This concerns her more than anyone."

Gramps caught the same thing Eli and I did. How does Mr. Crane know the panic room is downstairs?

"Ella needs to be with us!" Jamie's attention is pulled from his game and directly to Mr. Crane. "She's not safe."

"No, she's not safe," Mr. Crane agrees. "But I am someone even demons fear, Jamie. Ella is safe with me. I will protect her like she's my own daughter."

"Are you a bad man?"

"Some people think so, but I am a good man who does bad things and someone who will keep your sister safe. I swear it."

Jamie stares at him for a long time. "You remind me of my papa, but you're different. I see the bad in you, but you are kind, and Papa wasn't. If you let Ella get hurt, I will hurt you even if I have to wait a hundred years to get strong enough to do it."

Mr. Crane nods solemnly. "I would expect nothing else."

"Can we eat yet, Mama?"

"Almost." She looks frazzled and has that same deer-in-the-headlights look I've seen so many times on all our faces over the last year.

Jamie shrugs and goes back to his game, but we are all aware he's paying more attention than he appears to be. Kids are much more perceptive than people give them credit for.

"How about we table this discussion until after breakfast?" I ask and pour more scrambled eggs mixture into the pan.

"Sounds like a plan," Eli agrees. "Cecily, can you help me with the toast? I'll fill up the sheet pan and put it in the oven if you can operate the toaster."

She makes a face. "All we have is whole grain. I was going to pick up some regular bread after school."

"Whole grain won't kill you," Mom says. "You can put jelly or apple butter on it to mask the taste."

Whole grain bread tastes like cardboard, so I understand her not wanting to eat it. I wouldn't either if I had a choice.

The room settles down after that as we finish making breakfast. We move it all into the formal dining room so everyone has a place to sit.

The conversation is kept light because, after breakfast, it won't be all smiles and giggles. So I do my best to keep the looming threat of danger to the side and enjoy my breakfast.

Even if it all feels more than a little forced for Jamie's sake.

CHAPTER FIFTEEN

Once Jamie is settled downstairs with *Paw Patrol*, I come back upstairs to find everyone gathered in Gramps' office. Mr. Crane is over by the fireplace on the phone, while Gramps and Ethan are engrossed in the computer. Eli yawns when he sees me and gestures to the couch. I go over and fall beside him, grateful the couch is soft and comfy.

"How's Jamie?"

"Upset that I won't stay downstairs with him. I told him we'd watch cartoons as soon as we're done here. He's scared."

"That look is back in his eyes." Eli chews his bottom lip. "I don't like it. It took us weeks to get him to trust that's he's safe here and we're not going to get rid of him."

"There's not a lot we can do about it right now except keep reassuring him and popping in and out today to make sure he knows we're all still here."

"So...Leo?"

"I told her. It was time."

"Was she mad?"

"Nope, which shocked me. I'd have been pissed, but she took it in stride. She's a little overwhelmed, I think, but knowing about Leo and what he represents might be good to help her finish healing. He'll do everything to keep her safe, to make her feel safe, and I think that's the missing piece to her healing."

"You don't think we make her feel safe?"

"No, we do, but she knows us. Her issue is with strangers. I think getting to know him and understanding he's not going to hurt her might help her move past that hump in her healing process."

"Maybe." He grins after a moment. "She's not so happy with him right now. He's been very, very quiet, and Cecily is anything but. She's used to me and Jordan constantly talking and joking with her. I don't think she quite knows what to do with a more serious guy who's basically ignoring her."

"He's ignoring her?"

"He's watching. He knows he won't be able to smell the Chameleon. I told him everything we knew while we waited for Cecily. So he's using all his other senses to find things out of place, which takes a lot of his concentration. She'll get used to it."

Gramps looks up, and his eyes narrow. "What are you two over there whispering about? Not planning on doing something stupid, are you?"

"No, we were talking about Leo."

He grunts and goes back to the computer.

Ethan comes over and sits on the coffee table. It barely holds his weight. Not that Ethan's heavy or anything; he's just a big man and all muscle.

He's holding something in an evidence bag.

The note.

"Have you read this?"

I shake my head.

"Do you want to?"

"She doesn't need to see it," Eli says before I can answer. "She knows what it says. Seeing it will only make it worse."

"I can speak for myself, you know."

"I know." He reaches over and squeezes my hand. "Looking at the words will only make it worse. Trust me on this, please."

"Okay." I turn my attention to Ethan. "I need to talk to you about the dream I had the other night. I meant to tell you yesterday, but we all got sidetracked. And I had another one last night."

He lays the evidence bag to the side and focuses all his attention on me. I tell him about the first dream I had, and with each new detail, his face goes paler and paler.

"Do you know who the girl might be?"

"Yes, she's from Bluefield, Virginia. They found her boyfriend exactly as you described, but she wasn't found until about a week later."

"Where was she found?"

"On the steps of the police department."

"He does like to make a statement." No one had noticed Mr. Crane finish his phone call and listen in on our conversation. "The other cases I've been told about, are they the same when it comes to the dump sites?"

"Yes. Always somewhere very public."

"It's the same in all the other cases I've studied that are attributed to him as well. It's turned into his calling card."

"What's that?"

"It's their signature," Eli explains. "It's something unique to them that helps us identify their kills."

"You are your father's son." Mr. Crane smiles.

"You can't help but pick things up when you hear shop talk all the time."

"Emma said you wanted to play pro football. Are you sure about that? You'd make a fine detective."

"Yeah, I'm sure. I never really wanted to be in the family business, but Dad always made it sound like we didn't have a choice. I have that now, and I'm choosing football, which I'm good at and I love. Maybe after football, I might think about a job in law enforcement, but probably not."

"Daniel says you're more than good at the sport."

Eli shrugs.

Zeke digs into his pocket and pulls out his wallet. He looks through it a moment, then hands Eli a card. "That is the best sports agent in the business. She handles football players, specifically. She's fierce, and team owners and managers are afraid to piss her off. She'll be expecting your call when you're ready to declare for the draft."

Eli takes the card and looks at it for a full minute. "Thanks, Zeke. This means a lot."

"I take care of my family." He turns his attention to me. "Now, to you, *ma petite âme*. It sounds like the Chameleon has been watching you for quite some time if he's

211

picking other victims to test his methods on before coming for you. That is not good."

"No, no it's not," I agree. "The thought of someone watching me without me noticing is creepy."

"*Oui*, it is."

"So, what do we do?"

"I have been thinking." He strokes his chin and looks out the windows. "He's bold. I don't think you holing up in the house will stop him. He's already gotten close without triggering alarms. He's going to grow impatient when you don't leave the house. One of two things could happen. He'll pick another victim and simply wait for you to put your guard down. Or he'll come inside the house and try to take you. Alarm systems seem to be his area of expertise. He's gotten around the ones here, and Marco has some of the most sophisticated systems I've seen. It's better than my own, and the Chameleon still got around it."

"So, it won't matter where I am. When he wants me, he's going to get me."

"We're watching. He's not going to get near you."

"He did last night."

"The wolves weren't out in the woods." Ethan sighs heavily. "Cole has called a pack order. Every shifter in town, wolf or not, will be watching this house in shifts in their animal form. Threats have been made against his beta's mate. It's all hands on deck."

I've often wondered if it rankled Ethan when Cole Walker became the overall pack Alpha. Ethan is still in charge of his own pack, but Cole is like the king in these parts. All packs are his. He can overrule Ethan if he chooses.

"Things were so much simpler when I was just a normal girl moving from place to place as an Army brat."

Mr. Crane smiles. "I know the feeling of missing normalcy. I was only a boy when I drowned and woke up to see gruesome ghosts scaring me at all hours of the day and night until Mama and Papa built salt walls around the property. Children don't

213

understand not to disturb the line, especially active little boys who love running and climbing trees."

"You were forever a problem child."

The silky smooth voice startles us all. Gramps rises from his chair, anger etched in every line of his face.

"How did you get in here?" Gramps demands.

Silas flicks a nonexistent something from his white dress shirt. He's leaning against the fireplace, looking every inch the English lord his accent depicts. I can imagine him in Feudal England sitting in his study or by the fire. Only his black eyes mar the image. Those eyes are definitely not human.

"Hello, Ella Grace. I hear you are in need of my services." He smiles a Cheshire Cat smile, and it unnerves me.

"Your services are already bought and paid for." Zeke's sharp words bring a frown to Silas' face.

"Don't be rude, Ezekiel. I know the price has been paid. I am simply saying hello to Ella Grace."

"Again, how did you get in here?" Gramps snarls.

"Wards cannot keep me out, Marco. They can't keep me in, either, as Ezekiel will attest. Now, where is this southern hospitality I'm always hearing about? I'm not feeling the love."

"Does anyone need... Oh, I didn't hear the doorbell." Mom is staring at Silas, trying to figure out who he is.

"Mom, this is Silas. He's here to give me a tattoo."

"Several tattoos," Silas corrects.

"Absolutely not. You know how I feel about tattoos, Ella. The answer is no."

Silas arches a brow at Zeke.

"Molly, these are spelled tattoos to keep Ella safe." Ethan stands and goes over to her, taking her hands. "They are going to keep the ghosts from overwhelming her and making her relive their deaths. If it's not done, she could go mad from having their memories superimposed over hers day in and day out. It's for her safety."

"A tattoo, though, Ethan? Why a tattoo?"

"Because they are permanent and not easily manipulated. I know you hate the idea of them, but they are the best way to protect her. She's a Supernatural now, and spelled tattoos are a way of life for us."

She glares at us all and then stomps out of the room.

Wow. She's mad. My mother does not stomp out of rooms. Cecily and I have been sent to our rooms with no supper for doing that on more than one occasion.

"I'll go talk to her." Ethan shakes his head and leaves the room. Maybe having her mate around isn't going to be so bad if he can help her understand all the supernatural worldly things.

"Where do we do this?" Silas asks.

Gramps sighs. "The dining room. It has the biggest table."

"This is going to take hours," Silas warns. "Once I start, I won't stop. The girl must be quiet and not move. The designs and the spells are intricate. The slightest movement on her part could ruin the whole thing."

Gee, this sounds like a fun adventure.

"Uh, can we do this on my bed if it's going to take hours? I don't want to lie on a hard table that long."

Silas shrugs. "It doesn't matter to me."

"Eli, you stay in the room and watch that demon like a hawk. You've seen the tattoo before, so don't let him sneak something in that's not supposed to be there."

"Silas won't do that."

"And how do you know that, Ella Grace?" The demon's gaze centers on me.

"You made a deal for this, yeah?"

He nods.

"I've been reading up on demons. You have to honor your deals to the letter. Anything more or less can make the deal invalid, and I'm guessing you don't mess around with losing your deals."

He grins again. "I like her, Ezekiel. Can we keep her?"

"She's not ours to keep, Silas."

"The boy is ours, and since he claims her as family, that makes her ours too."

"No, Silas. You can't keep her." Mr. Crane is firm. "Do you want Emma to come looking for you?"

A real look of fear crosses his face. "My darling girl doesn't need to be brought into this."

"Then no more talk of keeping Ella."

"Fine," he says sullenly. "Go do what you need to do, Ella, and meet me upstairs in your room." He disappears.

"Where did he go?"

"He's somewhere in the house, I'm sure." Zeke shakes his head. "There's no controlling that demon."

"He's not going to be running around unattended in my home!" Gramps comes out from behind his desk and dashes out of the room, looking more than a little alarmed.

"Is he really a bad person?" I ask.

"I don't know. He is a demon, but he's a demon with a soul. He made a deal that allowed him to retain his soul. There is no other demon like him. Not even the oldest demon alive has a soul. I'm still not sure what that means, but I see glimmers of compassion and kindness from him. His soul is covered in ick, but I don't know how good or bad he really is."

"Are the other demons wary of him?"

"They should be, but demons, especially the first demons, are arrogant and think nothing and no one can harm them. Silas found a way to destroy one of them. They should be scared of him."

"Really? How did he do that?"

"That's a story for another day, *ma petite âme*. Best not to keep him waiting. He's right. This is going to take hours. Go see to your toiletries and then find him in your room. How are you with pain, by the way?"

"I survived the Army experimenting on me. A few tattoos will be easy."

He only smiles sadly before turning back to his phone.

What? It can't be worse than what I lived through.

Can it?

Eli shrugs when I look at him.

Crap.

CHAPTER SIXTEEN

Fifteen hours later, I'm eating my words. This is pain. Constant pain that I can't even pass out to escape. The buzzing of the tattoo needle sets my teeth to grinding. Sweat trickles down my face as Eli hums softly to try to distract me. Silas has threatened more than once to stitch my lips together to keep me from talking. I have the feeling he'd do it too.

I'm inked from my neck all the way down my back to my feet. The tattoos also wrap around my shoulders, thighs, legs and extend along my arms. Mom is going to be furious. I think she thought he meant a small tattoo here or there, not this complicated mess. Mr. Crane has come in a few times to check on us, reminding Silas to stick to the deal.

The demon slammed the door in Mr. Crane's face and told him to stay out the last time he came by.

"I know you."

The small voice stills Silas' hand. We all look to see Jamie watching from the door.

"Ah, young James. How are you?"

"What are you doing to my sister?"

"Giving her protection tattoos so the ghosts can't drive her mad."

"How do you know my brother?"

"He saved me from Papa the night Papa got really mad."

"I see you are here now with Ella. Is she taking good care of you?"

The boy nods. "Her and Cecily, and Mama and Gramps, and Eli, they take real good care of me. I get to eat all I want, and they don't hit me."

"Very good. Why aren't you asleep? Isn't it bedtime for you?"

"I had a nightmare. Ella lets me sleep in her bed when I have really bad ones."

"Can you sleep with your mama for tonight, young one? This is very intricate work, and the slightest movement can cause it to not work."

"I guess." His bare foot scuffs at the carpet.

"It's okay, Jamie. Mom won't let the bad dreams hurt you. I'll come check on you when we're finished."

His lip pudges out. Eli laughs and stands. "Come on, kid. Let's get you tucked in with Mama Molly. The sooner we get out of Silas' hair, the faster Ella can check on you." Eli takes his hand and leads him out of the room.

"What did he mean, that you saved him?" I ask before he can start in on the torture-fest again.

"Does it matter?"

"It does to me."

"I was here in town on business and was passing by their trailer. I heard the child screaming and looked in. His father was beating him, and I knew the boy would die if I didn't intervene. He was three. I'm surprised he even remembers me."

"What did you do?"

"I beat the man until he couldn't walk and cast a demon's curse on him so he couldn't shift and heal himself. Even his Alpha wouldn't be able to force the shift so he could heal. It was months before the curse wore off."

"Good. People like that don't deserve to live."

"You are a bloodthirsty little thing, aren't you?"

"Only when it comes to people who beat on kids."

"I agree, Ella Grace. People like that don't deserve to live. I make sure when they die, they land on my rack and spend an eternity paying for all the harm they did to children in life."

Mr. Crane is right. There is good in Silas even if that good is tainted with evil. He sounds positively thrilled to cause someone untold pain.

"Are you from England?"

"Why do you ask?"

"You sound like you belong in Feudal England."

He laughs and reloads his needle with spelled ink.

"So, are you English?"

"Yes, I am from England. Did the accent not give me away?"

"Anyone can fake an accent."

"True, but you can't fake being English."

"Sure you can."

"Only an American would think that."

"How long have you been in this body?" I ask. "I read demons have to jump bodies when the one they're in is close to expiring because of the damage housing a demon can do to it."

"You have done your research. Not many people know that."

"I like to read."

"Yes, I know. I noticed all the books." He tilts his head toward the four overflowing bookshelves. "Horror novels, by the looks of it."

"So?"

"So what?"

"How long have you had this body?"

"It's rude to ask a demon that. It's like asking a woman how old she is."

"I'm sorry, I didn't know."

"All this chit chat is not going to distract me from finishing your tattoos. My granddaughter uses the same tactics. It doesn't work for her, and it's not going to work for you."

Dang it. He's got my number.

A few minutes go by as he labors over the design he's creating on my back before he speaks again.

"I have never jumped bodies. It's part of the deal I made to become a demon. I am as I was when I was human. I did not wish to harm others just to walk among them in a form they wouldn't run screaming from. It is not something I wish known, though, Ella, so please keep it to yourself. I would prefer you not even inform Elijah. I'm trusting you with this secret."

"Why tell me?"

"You remind me of my darling girl. The two of you are as different as daylight from dark, but you have the same courageous spirit as Emma Rose. Both of you face danger. You run toward it instead of away from it. That deserves to be rewarded. There are not many on this Earth who would do it."

I'm not sure what to say to that, so I remain silent. It's not long before Eli returns, yawning for all he's worth.

"How much longer is this going to be?" he asks. "It's been almost sixteen hours."

"It takes time. The more you ask questions, the longer it will take me."

Eli sighs and rolls his eyes, but he shuts up.

It takes another three hours to complete the tattoos. Bandages are applied to certain areas where some of the more intricate design work was done.

"This was much easier than with Emma Rose." Silas packs away his ink and needles. "If she were as still and quiet as you, there would have been no reason to put her to sleep for the majority of my work."

"You could have put me to sleep?" I ask, outraged.

"Of course."

"Then why didn't you?"

"Why would I? You showed restraint in your pain and dealt with it beautifully."

"You enjoy pain, don't you?"

"I'm a demon, Ella. What do you think?"

Shaking my head, I start to respond, but he's gone when I look up. How does he do that?

"I didn't know he could put you to sleep. I would have had Zeke make him do it. I'm sorry."

"Nothing for you to be sorry for." I try to raise up and remember I'm naked. Eli has kept his eyes averted for the most part, but I'm very much aware of it now. "Uh, could you step out so I can get dressed?"

His eyes go wide, and he all but runs out of the room. It's cute. He forgot I was lying here without a stitch of clothing on. Just goes to show he has no romantic feelings for me, or he'd have reacted to that in a completely different way. As it is, his reaction is on par with that of a sibling. Sad, but true.

I'd rather have him as my friend and my family than not at all.

Sighing, I gently pick myself up off the bed and find the softest pajamas I own and a pair of underwear. It's difficult, but I manage it. I leave my hair up in the messy bun to keep it from aggravating the new ink on my neck. I'm afraid to look at it. I'll get Cecily to take photos later so I can study the designs in depth.

Going downstairs, I stop in the kitchen and find leftovers in the fridge. I'd smelled Mom's homemade beef stew all day as it cooked. I put some in a bowl and pop it in the microwave. While I'm waiting for it to warm, I pour myself a glass of milk. I've learned to drink milk with certain foods so as not to aggravate my acid reflux.

"Ella…I didn't realize you were done." Mom stares at me uncertainly from where she's just stepped out of the hallway leading to Gramps' office where the entrance to the panic room lies. "I was checking on the kids."

I nod but otherwise make no sound. I'm not sure what to say. I know she's angry about the tattoos, but if they can keep me from being overwhelmed or experiencing a ghost's death, then I'm all for it. And I'm a tattoo fan. I'd planned on getting one when I moved into the dorms. Maybe just somewhere she couldn't see it.

"I'm sorry about the way I reacted earlier." She starts to wring her hands, a sure sign she's nervous. "The thought of a tattoo on you while you're so young is distressing to me. It's permanent. You can't change your mind later, as teenagers are wont to do. You'll be stuck with it forever, and I wanted you and your sister to really think about this before doing something like that to your body."

"This isn't some whim, Mom. It's necessary. It'll keep my mind intact. I've already started to experience what Mr. Crane was talking about. I had a dream the other night of one of the stalker's victims. I felt everything she felt. I woke up with pain from the injuries she suffered. I don't want that, and if this will stop it, then I'm sorry you feel the way you do, but I'm going to protect myself."

She sighs heavily. "I hate the idea, but I understand it."

"Good. There may be more I need as my abilities grow and evolve. I don't know. You might end up with a daughter who has ink over every inch of her skin. Can you handle that?"

I don't actually think that, but it's better to prepare her for worst case now than deal with her reaction if it happens. I have no desire to be a walking, talking tattoo. I think it's gross. For those who enjoy that, that's fine. Good on them if they like that. I don't.

Mom actually flinches at the idea, but she doesn't go off on a tangent. "As long as it's for your safety, I will keep my opinions to myself."

She's still upset, but at least she's not storming off and slamming doors. A rare reaction from my very calm mother, and not one to be taken lightly.

"Are we okay?" I ask after a moment.

"Oh, honey, you never have to ask me that. You could go commit murder and I'd still be right there, standing beside of you because you're my child and I will love you no matter what."

She comes over and hugs me, which causes me to let out a sharp cry of pain. My back is one big mess of pain.

Mom jumps back, startled. "What?"

"The tattoo is up and down my backside. It hurts. Silas said it'll probably be really sore for a few days and to lie on my stomach when I sleep."

"I don't like that a demon did the tattoo."

"Silas is an odd one, all right. I'm not sure he's completely evil, but I'm not sure he's good either. I don't know how I feel about him in general."

"He's a demon, Ella. He can't be good."

"Jordan's father is a demon. Does that make Jordan not good?"

"No, of course not," Mom hurries to say, "but his mother is human. He has a conscience."

"Silas has a conscience. He still has his soul. He's the only demon alive who has one."

Mom frowns, unsure of what to do with that knowledge.

The microwave beeps, and I take my bowl of beef stew, wrapping a dish towel around it so I can handle the hot bowl.

"Is Jamie asleep?"

"Yes, he fell asleep about half an hour ago. He said you were going to come check on him when you were done."

"As soon as I eat this, I'll wake him up. He should go right back to sleep, though. Kid sleeps like the dead unless he's having nightmares."

"He was having dreams about the clown."

"Those are the worst for him."

"I know."

I sit at the table and start to eat, Mom watching me, and it makes me uncomfortable for some reason. It's like she's seeing straight through into my soul.

"I had so many plans for you girls."

"What do you mean?"

She comes to sit at the breakfast table with me. "When you were a little girl, I used to dress you up in pretty pink and purple clothes, ribbons in your hair, and imagine the day your father walked you down the aisle. You and Cecily both. You were forever a tomboy, though, always running after your father, and he encouraged you. Your love of dolls was replaced by your love of fishing and helping your dad work on the car. You were so independent, telling me exactly what you did and didn't like. My dreams changed for you. I encouraged your strong sense of self."

"Isn't it a good thing that I'm a strong, independent woman?"

"Yes, and I'm proud that I helped you grow into the person you are. I'm just sad that you won't have a normal life."

"Normal's overrated, Mom. Just because I see ghosts doesn't mean I can't have a semi-normal life. I'm still going to fall in love, get married, and have a few kids. I'll just do it while helping ghosts realize they need to cross over."

"And then there's Cecily. Mated to a shifter. What is her life going to look like?"

"She'll be more loved than anyone I know. Her every wish will be taken care of. Leo is going into pro football. She won't want for anything when it comes to money. How is that a bad thing?"

"I don't know." Mom drops her head into her hands. "Maybe coming to this town was a mistake."

"No, it wasn't. It was the best thing that ever happened to us. We have a home now. A place where we have friends and family. We're happy here, Mom. We saved Jamie. If I hadn't had that accident and woke up as a living reaper, he'd be dead. Can you honestly say you regret coming here, knowing we saved his life?"

What is wrong with her tonight?

"No, I will never regret that child. He's ours."

"Why all this morose talk? What's wrong?"

"I don't know. Sometimes I worry about the decisions I'm making for us and what might happen because of those decisions. What if everything I've done is wrong?"

"Mom, you do the best you can, and that's all anyone can ask for. You love us, and that matters more than any mistakes you might make. When you found out what Tony did and that Dad was fine with covering it up, you chose me and Cecily over him. That counts more than anything else. But Cec and I are growing up. You have to let us grow, make mistakes, and learn from them. Or not. We're going to do stupid things. All this supernatural stuff is no worse than living in gang territory in a city. You remember that one time we lived in Detroit? I never felt safe there, but I do here. Stalker and all, I still feel safe here. You gave us that."

"You really feel safe here? Even after everything that's happened to you and your sister?"

"I do. I can't speak for Cecily, but this is home, and I know the people here in this town will always make it feel like home. You worry too much, Mom."

"Just wait until you have children of your own, Ella Grace. There is no such thing as worrying too much, especially when your children wake up with new abilities."

"Don't speak such things. Remember what Great-Grandma used to say? Speak it and so shall it be."

"She also used to say Gremlins were real. I wouldn't put too much stock in those old sayings."

I finish my stew and put the bowl in the sink.

"I'm going to check on Jamie. Try to get some sleep, Mom, and trust in yourself and your decisions for our family. I do." I give her a hug and a kiss before heading upstairs to wake up my brother.

And then I'm sleeping for like a week.

CHAPTER SEVENTEEN

"Ella."

Eli's whisper brings me out of a dead sleep. His aqua eyes are bright in the darkness of my room. I sit up, and he puts a finger to his lips. Something's wrong. I can taste it in the air around us.

He hands me shoes and then motions for me to come with him. I throw the covers back, put the shoes on, and follow him out of the room without question.

The house is dark. It feels sinister. Probably because of how stealthy Eli's being. I don't like this.

We turn at the bottom of the stairs and go down the hallway to Gramps' office. Gramps, Mr. Crane, and Ethan are all in here, sitting in the dark. The blinds are down and the curtains closed.

What is going on?

The panic room door is open.

Why is it open? Gramps never leaves it open.

Ethan states the obvious. "We have a situation."

"Which is?" I ask when no one says another word.

"Someone was in the house."

"What?" I squawk.

Gramps motions to the panic room door. "I was restless and couldn't sleep. Decided to go check the windows and doors. When I came in here, the panic room door was open. I shut it before I went to bed."

"Maybe Mom or someone else…"

Gramps shakes his head. "I was the last one to bed. Everyone else was asleep, even Crane."

Mr. Crane must have slept over instead of going to the Blackburnes'.

"Is it…do you think it's him?"

"Ain't no one else it could be. He never sets off alarms. He's showing us he can get in whenever he wants."

"Does Leo know?"

Eli nods. "He's in Cecily's room. No one's touching your sister."

"Mom and Jamie?"

"Jamie's asleep in Molly's bed. I have someone I trust in there with them." Ethan rolls his head and shoulders. I hear the bones crack and the joints pop. I have the feeling he wants to shift, but he can't since he's in sheriff mode.

"So, what, he just walked in the front door and took a leisurely stroll through the house? Did he come in my room?"

The very thought freaks me out. He might have been watching me sleep. Or he could have touched me. I shudder at the thought.

"I don't know." Gramps sighs heavily. "I think we need to consider moving everyone. This house is not safe."

I was just telling Mom earlier how safe I felt here, and now Gramps is saying it's not safe for us to be here.

"I mean, if he's watching us, won't he know?"

"Possibly, but I'd rather move you and make it harder for him to find you than to leave you here and have him simply walk through the door and take you right out from under our noses. Been there, done that. Ain't doing it again."

"I've offered to take you all to my home in New Orleans." Mr. Crane puts his phone down. "I have resources there Marco doesn't have here. And a large security team to watch the house." He glances at Ethan. "No offense to your shifters, but they can't smell this thing. The security I can hire won't be relying on their noses, but on their ability to observe and find things out of the ordinary."

"Is running the best option?"

"Yes," all three men agree. Eli doesn't look like he agrees, but he's been outvoted.

"And if we are not in this town, we can utilize the abilities of Eli's father."

"But won't he come here if we involve him?" I don't want anyone in this town finding out who Eli really is and hate him for it. "The cases are here, so it stands to reason, he'd start here."

"I can convince James to come to New Orleans. If we remove what the Chameleon wants the most, he'll follow. He'll have no reason to remain in Jacob's Fork."

"And he wants me."

"Yes."

This sucks. This really sucks.

"I wish we had a better grasp on what he wants, but it's hard to get in his head when he's one step ahead of us." Mr. Crane sounds frustrated.

"What about getting in his victims' heads?"

All eyes turn to me, but it's Eli who speaks. "The last time you got near his victims, they tried to kill you."

"Only to keep me away from him."

No one looks thrilled with that answer. Look, I get why they did what they did. I don't think it was the smartest idea, but in their own way, they were trying to protect me. The guys don't see that, but I do.

"We're getting nowhere." Eli sighs. "I need to call Dad."

"Eli…"

"No, Ella. It's time. He was in the house with none of us aware of it. Zeke has his resources, and I have mine. We need to call Dad. He might have a bead on this guy none of the rest of us does. He hunts these kinds of creatures for a living. He might know more about what he is than we do."

"Wait, I forgot with everything going on and then the tattoo. There's something you should know."

Eli eyes me warily. I don't blame him. He's my Guardian Angel, and I tend to make that harder for him when I don't tell him things. But in all fairness, there was a lot going on.

"I've been having dreams of this cabin in the woods."

"Dreams?" Mr. Crane frowns.

I nod. "The cabin is built into the trees themselves, like the trees are a part of the structure or something."

They all remain quiet while I tell them about the two dreams I've had involving the cabin. "The graveyard in the back stretches as far as I could see, and I'm pretty sure it goes even farther. Some of the graves are really old, and some are newer. I've never seen or even read about anything like it."

"Neither have I," Mr. Crane mutters. "It sounds like you've developed a psychic link to either him or his victims. It might have happened when you died at the hands of said victims. Your soul attached to one of them."

"I had the first dream before that happened."

"I need to make some calls." Mr. Crane, phone in hand, walks out of the office.

Eli takes the cordless phone off the hook on the desk and dials a number he knows by heart. He'd told me once that his father never changed his work phone number. All of his kids knew it.

It only takes a moment for me to realize he has it on speakerphone. Gramps nods in approval.

"Malone," comes a voice gruff with sleep.

"Dad."

"Eli?" The alertness is instant. "What's wrong? Why are you calling at…four in the morning?"

"We have a situation here in town. It involves Ella."

"What's that girl gone and gotten herself into now?" The irritation is obvious, and I stiffen in response.

"My youngin' hasn't gone and gotten herself into anything." The deadly tone in Gramps' voice is strange to me. He's never used it on any of us.

"Who's that?"

"Marco McGreggor."

"Eli, do you have me on speakerphone?"

"Yeah, I do, Dad. Ella's right here too."

The line is quiet for a full minute.

"Maybe calling was a mistake. I should let you go back to sleep."

"No, don't hang up. You called for a reason. What is it?"

He certainly didn't apologize for what he implied about me.

"We have a serial rapist-slash-killer-slash stalker in town. What we know is he can't be tracked. Shifters can't smell him. He also has a knack for getting around security systems, and his vice is women with red hair. Have you ever come across anything like that over the years?"

"Yes. File 4121-79. I know it by heart. It was created the same month my unit came into existence."

"That was the same month the FBI was formed," Eli tells us.

Wow. They have an open file going back to the forties?

"How many victims?" Agent Malone asks.

"Seven that we know of."

"Why didn't you call earlier?"

"Because he doesn't want you anywhere near his home." It's my turn to speak up. "He's got a life here, with friends and family. If people knew you were his father, that would go away."

"It would not go away."

"Yes, it would. This is a town of Supernaturals. You hunt us, Dad. If people found out who I really am, I would lose all this."

"You and I disagree on this. You can always come home."

"No, he can't." Gramps' tone is forceful. "Just because the Angels aren't smiting any of you down don't mean they won't."

"Rhea placed her protection on all of us."

"And she ain't around all the time, is she? You don't know Angels like I do. They'd send someone they hate to smite you all and gladly let them die as a consequence. You might be willing take chances with his life, but I ain't."

James is quiet.

"Look, we're getting off track. What can you tell us about the Chameleon?" I ask. I don't want them to fight.

"Is that what you call him?"

"It's what Mr. Crane called him. He's been trying to find him since he killed his cousin ten years ago."

"Crane's looking into this?"

"Yes."

Eli fidgets, uncomfortable. "He's here."

"So, you'd rather have Crane there than me?" Under the anger, in his father's voice is hurt.

"No, but no one here will bat an eye at Zeke's presence. He's like us. He's a Supe."

"You are not a Supe, Eli."

"I am, Dad. I'm a Guardian Angel with all the abilities that go with it. If you can't accept that, then you can't accept me. I am one of the things you hunt."

"You're not evil."

"No, but then neither are the people in this town. You don't understand the difference between a good Supe and a bad one. To you, they're all just waiting to be hunted."

And we're off track again.

Gramps takes control of the conversation. "Malone, can you give us information or not? Without coming here."

"I'd need to see the files."

"You don't need to see the files to tell us what you already know about this creature," Marco counters.

Movement out of the corner of my eye catches my attention. I don't turn to it. Instead, I watch the shadows by the bookcase.

"We didn't have a name for it. Frankly, we weren't even sure it was the same creature. If it wasn't for the victims' red hair, we would have considered it copycats of one killer. Most copycats, however, will eventually break from the pattern of the one they're mimicking. They won't be able to help it. They'll want to put their own twist on the crime. It's simply how the mind of the depraved works."

Another slight shift in the shadows, almost like someone is standing there and flinching. Or laughing.

"From what I've read, he's moved not only state to state, but country to country, killing no more than eight to ten in each place he goes. His dump sites are always public and either a snub to the police or to the victim's family. The victims are brutally beaten and raped for days before they die. He likes to dismember them or mutilate them or both."

"Is that all you know, Dad? That's exactly what Zeke told us."

He doesn't say anything.

"Look, this thing killed Zeke's cousin who he said was more like a sister. He named Hilda after her. He wants him brought to justice as badly as we do. It's set its sights on Ella. He was in the house tonight, and none of us knew it. We need all the information we can get to stop it before it gets her."

There is a definite shift in the shadows. Stepping away from the desk, I move closer to the corner where something's off. It doesn't look any different than it did before. The furniture hasn't been moved. The walls are the same. The painting is… Wait. I look closer. The frame of the painting is slightly off, like a section of it is superimposed over the rest of it. That's weird.

"Ella, what are you…"

Before I can say a word, something detaches from the wall and runs past us, blurring as it moves. There's a shout, and we all run to see where the thing went.

Zeke's sprawled on the floor, and the front door is open.

Eli goes to make sure he's okay while Gramps shuts and locks the door.

"Was that…" I can't even bring myself to say it.

"I think so." Gramps looks at Eli. "He okay?"

"I'm fine, thank you." He looks at the door. "Where did it come from?"

"It was in the office. I thought I saw movement out of the corner of my eye and went to look. Everything looked the same except for an edge of the picture frame. One section looked like it was layered, one piece on top of the others. Before I could say anything, it detached from the wall and ran."

"It knocked me down on its way out the door."

"Are you sure it went outside?"

251

"I saw it go."

Letting out a breath, I try to center myself. Some of my calm is finally staring to break. This thing was in my house. It was watching us and listening to our plans.

"We can't go to New Orleans. He heard us."

Zeke's expression turns murderous.

"We need to go somewhere, though. If it can get in this easily, none of us will be safe."

"I think we need to separate Ella from the rest. I think they'll be safer if the creature is tracking her and not them." Zeke looks pained at even suggesting it, but I know he's right. Mom is going to pitch a fit, however.

"Agreed," Gramps says. "We can send Molly, Cecily, and Jamie to New Orleans just to be safe. Those bodyguards of yours had better keep my family safe."

"They will," Zeke promises. "Now, what to do with Ella?" He taps his chin. "I own several properties across the US. All of them have top-of-the-line security."

"Ella, that cabin you talked about, do you think it's here?"

"I didn't recognize anything remotely similar to our mountains, but it was deep in the woods. I might not have recognized it."

"Come on. Dad's probably having a heart attack right about now." Eli helps Mr. Crane up, and we all go back into the office. He picks up the phone from where it dropped on the floor. "Dad, you still there?"

"Where else would I be when the phone is dropped and you all start running? What happened?"

Eli explains, and Mr. Crane looks more and more concerned. "I think I'm going to ask Alecia to go and stay with your mother, your sister, and your brother in New Orleans. I'd rather have a witch with them who can deal some damage. Call it another layer of protection."

Gramps nods. I'm not sure Mom is going to be so amenable to this little plan of theirs, even if there is wisdom in it.

"You said there were seven deaths?" Agent Malone asks.

"Yes."

"That would make Ella victim number eight. He's at his sweet spot. Getting her out of town might actually prevent another death. I agree with you on that. Why don't you bring her here to Charlotte, Eli? My team is based here, and we can work the case."

"No. People in Charlotte think I'm dead. They went to my funeral, Dad, including every member of your team. Going there is out of the question."

"We could give you a glamour and they wouldn't know it was you."

"I'd still sound like me. The ones who knew me would recognize the glamour for what it is. I'm not risking my life, Ava's life, Caleb's life, or Benny's life. We've worked too hard to be able to at least talk to each other for me to go and ruin that now. I lost my family once. Don't ask me to do that again, Dad, because I won't."

"You're right. I'd rather be able to talk to you than for the Angels to take you or one of your siblings away. I'm not going to risk my children's safety."

Somehow, I don't believe him. Call me biased, but I think he would risk his children because he believes he'd win the fight in the end. I may be the only one who thinks that, though.

"What if I come to wherever you go? I'll only bring Caleb and the new members of my team who don't know you. You'd still need a glamour because your photo is on my desk, but I'd be able to be there to protect you."

"It's not a bad idea," Mr. Crane says. "It would need to be somewhere you've never worked a case or gone hunting with your boys."

Eli snorts. "Then we're sunk. We've been all over this country."

"Have you ever been to Ireland?"

We all turn to Gramps. "What?" I ask, not sure I heard him right.

"I own a house in Ireland, about an hour outside Dublin. I have the same types of security systems there as I do here, both technological and magical. Do you have a passport, Ella?"

I nod. "We all have one because we moved so much as we were growing up. I got it renewed right before we came to Jacob's Fork because Dad thought he was going to be based overseas again. We didn't find out about West Virginia until three days before we were supposed to board the plane to London. I was actually looking forward to going there. I wanted to see Big Ben and the guards at Buckingham Palace."

Gramps smiles. "Perhaps we can do a layover in London and let you see them."

"Mom's not going to agree to this."

"Your mother will put her children's safety over her own fears. I'll go wake her up. You need to pack. You and Eli. Just a small carry-on, maybe three changes of clothes. We'll buy whatever else you need when we get there."

"Dad, did you hear that?"

"I did. Have Marco send me the address and tell him to use a secure line to do it. I'll meet everyone there."

They say goodbye, and Eli looks unsure. I hate that look.

"What?" I ask.

"I guess I never thought I'd get sucked back into another investigation or hunting trip with Dad again. He has this way of making me think like him instead of for myself."

"That's why you have me. I won't let him do that. I'll remind you of who you are."

"Promise?"

"I swear."

Sighing, he nods, and we go upstairs to pack.

CHAPTER EIGHTEEN

The house is abuzz with activity a few hours later. Mom argued for the better part of an hour but gave in when Mr. Crane asked if she'd rather put all her children's lives in danger. He assured her he'd go with us to help protect me while his family in New Orleans would protect them. She's not happy, but at least she's not being stubborn about it.

We did have to tell her the Chameleon got in the house while we were sleeping. She did not appreciate that any more than I did. It freaked Cecily out the most, but given she's experienced what some of the previous victims of the Chameleon had been through, I knew it would. Frankly, I didn't want to tell her, but she needed to know. Leo had to walk out of the house when I told them that. He didn't want her to associate him with anger and violence.

I would bet money the creature never went in Cecily's room. Leo spent the night in her room, sitting in a chair facing the door. I doubt he even slept. My, Jamie's, or Mom's rooms? He might have gone in one of those. Even one of the guys'. Maybe not Ethan's. If Ethan stayed over. He would have felt the shift of energy in the room, I think, if someone were standing over him. He's very aware of his surroundings.

I look around my room, trying to decide if there's anything I can't live without for a few days. Or weeks. Not sure which at this point. Mom called the school and explained what was going on. We'll all be doing remote work while away so our grades don't suffer. We only have a few months of school left, and then Eli and I will be graduating.

Running from a stalker one month and graduating the next. I really hope my life calms down. Can't I just deal with a mundane ghost who doesn't understand they're dead every once in a while, instead of monsters like the Sandman, the Army, and now this Chameleon.

I sneeze and remember I haven't taken my meds. Honestly, I think I was too late for the Tamiflu. The doctor sent antibiotics as well just in case I was too late for the flu medicine to work and as a preventative measure against chest infections or pneumonia developing from the flu. Better safe than sorry, he said, especially since my immune system is still a little rundown from everything I've been through this last year.

If I survived the Army, I'll survive this.

At least that's what I've been telling myself. My calm from before is fading, and a deep fear is taking root. I'm not sure what changed other than he got in the house undetected. I mean, he could have done that the first time he was here. He chose to break in, and I think that was more to inspire fear than because he had to do it.

Chameleon is definitely a good name for whatever he is. He literally blended in with the wall, the chair, and the painting so well, none of us noticed he was there. If it hadn't been for that one little blip in the painting's frame, we wouldn't have known. I'd have told myself I was seeing things, and that would have been that. As it is, I'm examining everything I come into contact with because I can't know for certain it's not him.

"Hey, you about ready?" Eli sticks his head in. "Gramps wants us all to go to the airport at the same time. He wants no one left behind."

"Yes, just taking one last look around to make sure there's nothing I need."

"We'll get you whatever you need once we get there."

I sigh heavily. "I don't like this."

"Me either, Shortcake, but it's for the best."

"You don't sound like you believe that any more than I do."

"I'm worried about the Chameleon, but I have no doubt we'll catch him. My father is very good at what he does. It's more that I'm worried the old me will resurface. You might not like him as much as you do this version of me."

"I think you're worrying way too much. And I'll like whatever version of you is around. You're my best friend, and besties will always sort out each other."

He tries to smile, but it falls flat.

"Going somewhere?"

We both jump at Silas' voice.

"Do you always just pop into people's rooms unannounced?"

"Yes, now answer my question."

"We're going to Ireland to try to pull the Chameleon away from Ella's family."

"The what?" He swings his head toward Eli, his long, dark locks swinging. I never really thought long hair looked good on men, but it suits Silas.

"Did you not listen to any of the conversation going on in the house while you were inking Ella?"

Silas glares at my bestie. "As you said, I was busy inking Ella. The slightest distraction could have ruined the design."

"Fair," Eli says and explains what we've been dealing with.

"I did not realize they were still active," Silas says softly and looks at me, his eyes concerned. "When they set their sights on something, they always get it."

"You know the creature?" Eli asks.

"No, but I know of them. They're called the Invisibles because of their ability to appear invisible, but I think Chameleon is a far better name, as these creatures share some traits with a chameleon."

"Is there a way to kill it?"

Silas' lips thin, and then he's gone.

"Does he always do that?"

"Pretty much. It aggravates Hilda to no end."

"Gramps is not going to like him just dropping in whenever he wants."

"Zeke hates it, but Silas will do what Silas wants without any consequences. Wards can't stop him. I've seen him walk through death wards without so much as a flinch."

"Wouldn't it be nice to be able to appear and disappear at will?"

"That's exactly what Hilda says."

"Silas is her grandfather, isn't he?"

Eli nods.

"Then maybe one day she'll be able to do that."

"For the love of God, don't put that in her head. She'll drive us all mad trying to test it daily. God help us if she figures out how to do it. Neither Dan nor I can do it, and she'd end up somewhere we couldn't get to her."

Smiling, I can imagine Emma Crane sitting on the floor, trying her hardest to mimic her grandfather's disappearing act. And then all the men in her life running around trying to stop her.

"Here we are."

Silas is back, and he's holding a book so old, it looks like the barest touch will cause it to fall apart.

"I knew I still had this. It's everything that's known about The Invisibles. At least known when it was written."

He goes to hand it to me, but Eli stops him. "What do you want for it?"

"Nothing."

Eli's eyes narrow, but mine don't. Silas has helped me before.

"Why would you give this to us without wanting something in return?"

He smiles. "Maybe one day, I will tell you, Ella Grace, but for now, trust that I mean you no harm and only wish to help."

I take the book carefully. It feels fragile in my hands. "Is this thing going to fall apart?"

"No. I put a spell on it to keep it intact."

Setting it on the bed, I open the book and look through it. It's in a language I don't know. "What language is this?"

"It's the demon language, of course."

"I can't read this."

"Ezekiel can."

"Will they let us through customs with this?" Eli asks, coming over, curious to see what's inside.

"I didn't think of that. I'll take it and leave it at your destination. You'll be able to read through it at your leisure."

"Or at Zeke's leisure." Eli shakes his head and closes the book. "I don't know why you're doing this, but thank you, Silas."

"You're very welcome, Guardian." Silas picks the book up and looks at me. "Ella Grace, be careful, be alert, and if you need me, just call for me, and I'll come."

"No…" He's gone before Eli can get the words out. "I don't like that he's taken such an interest in you."

"Neither do I, but I'm not turning down his help."

"We need to go. Gramps is shouting for us to get downstairs. We'll tell him about the book on the way to the airport."

I nod and look around my room one last time, unsure when I'll see it again.

Taking a deep breath, I pick up my small bag and follow Eli out of the room, unsure of what awaits once we land in Ireland, but hopeful we'll be able to stop the Chameleon before he does any more damage.

ABOUT THE AUTHOR

So who am I? Well, I'm the crazy girl with an imagination that never shuts up. I LOVE scary movies. My friends laugh at me when I scare myself watching them and tell me to stop watching them, but who doesn't love to get scared? I grew up in a small town nestled in the southern mountains of West Virginia where I spent days roaming around in the woods, climbing trees, and causing general mayhem. Nights I would stay up reading Nancy Drew by flashlight under the covers until my parents yelled at me to go to sleep.

Growing up in a small town, I learned a lot of values and morals, I also learned parents have spies everywhere and there's always someone to tell your mama you were seen kissing a particular boy on a particular day just a little too long. So when you get grounded, what is there left to do? Read! My Aunt Jo gave me my first real romance novel. It was a romance titled "Lord Margrave's Deception." I remember it fondly. But I also learned I had a deep and abiding love of mysteries and anything paranormal. As I grew up, I started to write just that and would entertain my friends with stories featuring them as main characters.

Now, I live in Huntersville, NC where I entertain my niece and nephew and watch the cats get teased by the birds and laugh myself silly when they swoop down and then dive back up just out of reach. The cats start yelling something fierce...lol.

I love books, I love writing books, and I love entertaining people with my silly stories.

Facebook:
https://www.facebook.com/authorApryl
Baker

Twitter:
https://twitter.com/AprylBaker

Website:
http://www.aprylbaker.com

Bookbub:
https://www.bookbub.com/authors/apryl-
baker

Wattpad:
http://www.wattpad.com/user/
AprylBaker7

Newsletter:
https://www.subscribepage.com/j5d0z5

Facebook Fan Page:
https://www.facebook.com/groups/
AprylsAngels

Instagram:
https://www.instagram.com/apryl.baker

Amazon:
https://goo.gl/b1br13